Confetti & Confusion

Confetti & Confusion

DAISY JAMES

CANELO

First published in the United Kingdom in 2018 by Canelo

This edition published in the United Kingdom in 2019 by

Canelo Digital Publishing Limited
57 Shepherds Lane
Beaconsfield, Bucks HP9 2DU
United Kingdom

A CIP catalogue record for this book is available from the British Library.

Print ISBN 978 1 78863 414 4
Ebook ISBN 978 1 78863 019 1

Look for more great books at www.canelo.co

Printed and bound in Great Britain by Clays Ltd, Elcograf S.p.A.

To everyone who loves chocolate — may your tastebuds ever tingle!

Chapter One

'Hello, everyone, and welcome to Claudia Croft's Paradise Cookery School here on the gorgeous island of St Lucia. I'm Amelia Harper and this week, along with my co-presenter, Ella Johnson, I'll be demonstrating a whole host of delicious recipes before giving you all the opportunity to try them out for yourselves under our supervision.'

Millie inhaled a deep breath to steady her rampaging nerves, but her heart continued to hammer out a symphony of fear, sending spasms of electricity out to her fingertips. How had she got herself into this? Overseeing the kitchen renovations for celebrity cookery book writer and chef Claudia Croft was one thing, but presenting one of her prestigious courses was quite another. As she stared out at the eager faces in front of her she pulled herself together. What was she so worried about? She could do this!

'At the request of Imogen, our fabulous bride-to-be, Claudia has designed a week of personalised tutorials that she's called Chocolate and Confetti, crammed with mouth-watering chocolate-inspired recipes, all of which you'll be able to taste-test at the end of each day.'

'Yay!' squealed Gracie, the youngest member of the pre-wedding hen party at eight years old, clapping her hands and pogoing up and down on the spot in her two-sizes-too-big-for-her apron. A wave of laughter rippled around the room as Imogen patted her niece's blonde curls affection-ately.

'Also, as a special treat, a good friend of ours, Lottie Bedford, has designed a range of delicious cocktails made from locally sourced ingredients, including a really delicious recipe that contains the flesh of the cocoa pods you see growing in the villa's grounds.'

'Mmm!'

This time the sigh of pleasure came from the adult members of the group, particularly Imogen's sister, Karen, and her bridesmaids, Carla and Harriet, whilst her mother, Julia, rolled her eyes at them.

'Don't worry, there'll be a few alcohol-free versions to choose from, too. Lottie really is a maestro at mixing exotic flavours. Ella and I had hoped that she would be with us this week but she's been promoted to manager of the Purple Parrot bar in Soufrière after the proprietor had a run-in with the local police. So, shaking cocktails will be a new skill that we can learn together.'

Millie glanced around at the six chocoholics who had chosen to spend the week before Imogen's glamourous nuptials learning how to create all things cocoa-related instead of indulging in the more traditional exploits of raucous hen parties down in the bars and restaurants in Soufrière, the former St Lucian capital at the bottom of the hill. Not only would they be turning their hands to producing desserts, cakes and patisserie containing their beloved bean, but Millie also intended to explain how the chocolate they were using was produced from the tiny nibs found inside the weird purple-brown pods that grew on the trees in the villa's extensive grounds.

'So, I hope you all have a fun and productive week but that you also leave the Paradise Cookery School with a treasure trove of new recipes in your repertoire with which to impress your friends when you return home.'

'If you can teach Imogen to bake anything that isn't tinged with the aroma of burnt tyres, or completely caramelised to a crisp, then I'll be happy!' laughed Julia, smirking at her daughter, her affection apparent for all to see.

'Hey! Is it my fault that I prefer to support the products made by our friends at Patisserie Valerie and Hotel Chocolat?' Imogen retaliated, a wide grin splitting her cheeks.

'Okay, so I thought I would start by demonstrating a couple of my favourite childhood recipes passed down from my French grandmother – chocolate truffle tortes with hazelnut brittle and chocolate and cherry madeleines.'

Millie smoothed her trembling palms over the front of the pale-lemon apron that had been embroidered with Claudia's famous CC logo. Her knees shook a little and she was grateful she'd had the good sense to ditch her heels for a pair of sequinned flip-flops. However, as soon as she began to weigh out the ingredients, her anxiety vanished and the next three hours passed in a whirl of frenzied activity. She even had to admit that she was enjoying herself; after all, baking had always been her go-to activity to escape the grenades that life had thrown in her path.

When Claudia had asked her to step into her shoes at the last minute, Millie's first reaction had been to panic. She had been more than happy to temporarily swap her job as a pastry chef in a tiny patisserie in London to oversee the upgrade of the villa's kitchen after Claudia broke her leg in a horse riding accident. It had been the perfect opportunity to escape the heartache caused by the breakdown of her relationship with Luke and spend some time in the Caribbean sunshine. However, she had never in her wildest dreams thought she would still be there two weeks later, wearing the course presenter badge!

So, here she was, standing in front of six well-heeled women – in both senses of the word – all of whom were expecting to be guided through the labyrinth of culinary excellence by the celebrated TV chef and cookery writer. She had tried to refuse, but by the time Claudia's doctors had forbidden her to travel, the hen party guests had already arrived at the luxury boutique hotel where the wedding of the year was taking place at the end of the week, and it was too late to cancel. Millie didn't want to let Claudia down – or to disappoint the bridal party – so, against her better judgment, she had reluctantly agreed to step into the breach.

As the proud owner of a Michelin star, she *did* have the necessary culinary qualifications to deliver the course, and she and Ella *had* spent the previous two weeks triple-testing every single recipe on the itinerary. Even so, she was terrified that Claudia's very first Chocolate & Confetti course would be a flop, that the Paradise Cookery School would receive dreadful reviews, which in turn would jeopardise any plans Claudia had for future courses. Whilst that scenario would be upsetting for Claudia, who adored her Caribbean home, because her main place of business was located in a manor house in the Cotswolds, it wouldn't affect her business too much. What Millie was most concerned about was how the failure would affect Ella, her co-host and newfound friend, whose long-held dream to run a cookery school was about to come true. Everything rested on Millie and she had to give it her best shot.

At lunchtime, the group broke from their activities to gather on the veranda and feast on a kaleidoscope of Caribbean-inspired salads prepared by Ella before resuming their positions behind their respective workstations for the afternoon tutorial.

'I'll now pass the culinary baton over to Ella, who is going to demonstrate how to make mini chocolate-orange roulades filled with marmalade made from the oranges that are grown right here on the Croft estate. Then, to end the day with a sizzle, we'll make one of Ella's signature recipes that her son, Henri, swears are the best he's ever tasted – chilli-chocolate brownies.'

'Yay!' squealed Gracie. 'I love chocolate brownies!'

'You might want to add a little less chilli to your own recipe!' laughed Ella, taking Millie's place at the marble-topped demonstration bench, every inch the Caribbean cook extraordinaire.

That day, in honour of the occasion, Ella's ample proportions were enhanced by a tropically inspired kaftan scattered with sequin and gemstone embellishments, and a necklace made of hand-crafted wooden beads the size of quail's eggs with matching earrings. Millie smiled; her co-presenter clearly lived by the mantra that excess was better when it came to technicoloured wardrobe choices.

Listening to Ella's melodic Caribbean lilt as she explained the importance of lightness of touch when it came to making sponge cake, Millie's heart gave a squeeze of gratitude for her friend's expertise and calm professionalism in contrast to her own tendency towards culinary clutter. She adored Ella – with her penchant for exotic spices and habit of dispensing blunt, yet level-headed advice. Her knowledge of Caribbean cookery was extensive, embroidered over the years with a variety of influences from Creole to French, from Spanish to American. Millie knew she couldn't have done any of this without her support.

'Take care when slicing the oranges,' cautioned Ella.

'Yes, Immie darling, we don't want the bride trussed up in bandages on her wedding day, do we? Not exactly the must-have accessory for the theme I have planned for the wedding,' said Julia, who had reluctantly swapped her Italian-designed cropped jacket for one of Claudia's signature pale-lemon aprons. With her towering Louboutins, her whole ensemble screamed the sartorial equivalent of 'look at me!' Yet her intensely groomed caramel bob had already succumbed to the ambient humidity, and her early morning visit to the hotel's hairdressers had turned out to be a pointless exercise. 'Never mind spoiling the photographs!'

'Oh, Mum! I wish you'd relax over the whole "attention-to-detail" thing you have going on. We're supposed to be enjoying ourselves, not stressing over the wedding arrangements. We have a wedding planner to do all that.'

'But she's useless. She was over an hour late for our appointment yesterday morning and when she did eventually turn up she'd forgotten to bring the floral samples with her. And would you believe that when I asked about the butterflies she looked at me as though I was crazy. I bet she hasn't even ordered them. Honestly, Imogen, I don't know what we are paying her for…'

'Mum, I keep telling you, Alex and I just want a laid-back wedding day, surrounded by the people we love in a relaxed and stress-free atmosphere. I definitely won't be devastated if we don't get to release a kaleidoscope of butterflies after we've exchanged our vows, or if the confetti doesn't have our picture on it. In fact, why can't we have rice? That's what I wanted in the first place.'

'That's what peasants do at weddings!' shot back Julia, combing her fingers through her straw-like hair.

'No it's not,' laughed Imogen, tossing jagged lumps of orange peel into the jam pan that was on the hob she shared with her mother, whose own fruit segments were perfectly sliced. 'I really don't understand why we couldn't have had a quiet country wedding at home. I loved the idea of the village fête theme Karen suggested.' Imogen smiled at her sister, who was concentrating on showing Gracie how to grate her chocolate without also grating her fingers. 'Hoopla, juggling, guess how many sweets in the jar, a huge meringue-like marquee, pastel bunting floating in the breeze. I think our friends would have loved that!'

'Don't be facetious, dear. It doesn't suit you.'

Millie left the bride's family to their obviously well-rehearsed argument and moved on to the adjacent marble-topped workstation where Imogen's two bridesmaids were attempting a version of Ella's chilli-chocolate brownie recipe. A giggle, followed by a very unladylike snort of laughter, erupted from Carla as she tried to conceal the fact that her cheeks were bulging like an over-zealous hamster, obviously having started early on the taste-testing part of the day. Not to be outdone, Harriet was squirting chocolate buttercream into her mouth from a piping bag. Every spare inch of their countertop was scattered with culinary debris – splodges of butter, snail trails of powdered sugar and dots of melted chocolate, not to mention the jumble of discarded implements in the sink.

Millie smiled. She was the last person to chastise anyone for making a mess in the kitchen, having been told on more than one occasion that she could bring chaos to an empty room by many a friend and colleague, and more recently by Zach Barker.

Her spirits edged up a notch further when she thought of Claudia and Tim Croft's prickly estate manager whom she had crossed spatulas with when she arrived at the villa two weeks ago. From a difficult start, when she had mistakenly thought Zach was the gardener rather than their highly qualified estate manager on secondment from their country manor house in the UK, they had gone on to form an unexpected friendship. In the space of a few days, he had achieved what her friend Poppy back home in London had failed to do in six months — forced her to put her disastrous relationship history into perspective.

So what if Luke had ditched her at their engagement party, in front of all their friends and family, and run off into the sunset with her best friend's mother? That was his decision and there was nothing she could do about it. No amount of tears and painful soul-searching would change the situation, or lessen the embarrassment. With his special brand of sarcastic wit, Zach had helped her to face the demons that had taken up residence in her mind and serve them with an eviction notice. They hadn't left yet, but they had packed their bags and ordered a taxi. She was even starting to come to terms with the fact that Luke and Donna were expecting their first child in a few months' time.

Satisfied that Carla and Harriet had everything under control, Millie sauntered back to the demonstration bench. She allowed her thoughts to linger briefly on the previous day when she and Zach had shared a kiss beneath the palm trees and a pleasurable swirl of desire meandered through her veins. However, mingled with the undoubted pull of attraction was a nugget of uncertainty. Did she really want a holiday fling? Even if it was with someone who made every one of her senses zing with excitement and anticipation whenever they were together? Because, sadly, that was all it could be — at the end of her brief sojourn in paradise, she would return to her life in London and it was unlikely they would see each other again.

An enticing fragrance of warm sugar and chocolatey sponge cake floated towards Millie's nostrils, dragging her back to the present.

'Okay, everyone, time for that part of the day I know you have all been waiting for.' Millie cast a smile in the direction of Carla, who was busy photographing everyone's masterpieces with her beloved Pentax camera. 'Let's taste our creations!'

She arranged the products of the group's labour on four huge china platters decorated with Claudia's signature logos. The first showcased a perfect selection of the patisserie she had made that morning, along with the miniature chocolate-orange roulades covered with chocolate ganache and the chilli-chocolate brownies baked by Ella. The second plate held the cakes made by Imogen and Julia, the third by Karen and Gracie, and the last one was piled high with the offerings belonging to Harriet and Carla.

'Well done, everyone. These all look absolutely amazing!' declared Ella, her mahogany eyes sparkling with pride.

'You're too kind,' laughed Harriet. 'My roulades look like a steamroller has reversed over them! I'm not sure I actually *want* to eat them.'

'You're right — we do initially taste with our eyes. But in my opinion, the most important part of any bake is its aroma and its taste. Don't forget — the Chocolate and Confetti course is not a competition. It's an opportunity for you to learn new skills and improve on old ones. By the end of the week — when we will be tackling chocolate eclairs and profiteroles — I promise you'll be making patisserie fit to grace any Parisian store.'

'I wouldn't bet on it,' murmured Carla, eyeing her caramelized madeleines with disdain.

'Okay. Let's dig in!'

'Mmm. Gracie, darling, your chilli-chocolate brownies are simply delicious,' said Karen, holding her hand under her chin to catch any crumbs, smiling widely at her daughter.

'Thanks, Mum. I think these biscuits are the best, though.'

Amid the cacophony of animated conversation, coupled with the soft strains of calypso music emanating from the radio in the corner and the ever-present backing track of the cicadas, everyone in the hen party indulged in their favourite pastime – eating chocolate in all its guises.

'Oh my God, Millie. These have got to be *the* most delicious chocolate tortes I've ever tasted!' declared Imogen, reaching for a second and trying to stuff it into her mouth whole.

'A little decorum, darling!'

'This is the best hen week ever,' continued Imogen, ignoring her mother's chastisement. 'Who else gets to indulge their love of all things cocoa-related *and* feast their eyes on that magnificent view at the same time?'

The women gravitated to the sun-bleached wraparound veranda overlooking the Soufrière bay. Millie took a moment to appreciate the most spectacular example of nature's artwork. To their left, the Gros Piton and Petit Piton mountains rose from the Caribbean Sea like the spikes of a slumbering dinosaur, their peaks melting into a soft eiderdown of cloud, their emerald interiors seemingly replete with legends, fairy tales and pirate stories. All this verdant beauty was set against the deep sapphire of the ocean, its surface dotted with tiny flecks of multi-coloured sails, cruise ships laden with tourists, and cargo ships trailing a ripple of cappuccino froth in their wake.

'It *is* beautiful, isn't it?'

'Stunning. I've had an amazing day, Millie. It's been something that everyone can get involved in. I know Mum has had a fantastic time, but so has Gracie. Thank you so much for everything.'

'You're welcome. I'm sorry Claudia wasn't able to be here.'

'Gosh, don't apologise. Okay, when Mum booked the course we were expecting the celebrated Claudia Croft to regale us with juicy anecdotes about her TV show and teach us a few of her personal techniques, but you and Ella have been fantastic. I can't believe you're a pastry chef at a tiny patisserie in Hammersmith. Why aren't you working in a prestigious restaurant in the West End, shouting about your Michelin star accolade from the rooftops?'

'Oh, well, you know, life gets in the way of our dreams sometimes. Maybe one day…'

Now was definitely not the time to divulge the details of her relationship catastrophe, especially not to Imogen, who was about to exchange her wedding vows in a no-expense-spared ceremony on the lawns of an elegant five-star hotel, courtesy of her architect fiancé, Alex Watson. But Imogen was right. She shouldn't be hiding in London whilst Luke continued to run the restaurant in Oxford where they had jointly achieved the coveted Michelin star.

However, the shock revelation of the identity of Luke's girlfriend had meant she'd had to get away. She hadn't been able to deal with the shame, and despite finding out that her best friend Frankie had been as much in the dark about Luke's betrayal as she had been, she had chosen to run away, to hot-foot it to London where she had landed her job at Étienne's Parisian Patisserie.

But now, after her extended stay in the Caribbean, she had mixed feelings about returning to her studio home amid the chimney pots and TV aerials. She loved the hustle and bustle of her new life in the capital, and the fantastic nights out with her fellow pastry chef and new best friend, Poppy. What she wasn't looking forward to were the dark, leaden skies, the terrible traffic fighting for supremacy on the city's streets, or the pressure from her family to fulfil her dream of one day running her own restaurant again after the heartache Luke's infidelity had caused.

A wave of tiredness rolled over her, her feet ached, but her overwhelming feeling was one of exhilaration. Now that the first day of the Paradise Cookery School had been a success, she couldn't wait to showcase what she and Ella had planned for the rest of the week. Maybe she *could* change her life by branching out into cookery demonstrations when she returned home? A splash of excitement burst into her chest at the prospect.

'I wish Alex and I were getting married here instead of up at the hotel,' mused Imogen, gazing down at the rectangle of aquamarine glittering in the sunshine on the terrace below the veranda, where Julia was stretched out on a sun lounger with a cocktail she had invented herself. 'It's exactly what Alex and I want. Small, intimate, friendly.'

'I think Claudia does have plans to offer guests of the Paradise Cookery School the chance to experience the full package; accommodation, gourmet meals and maybe even guided tours of the cocoa plantation. Since she bought the estate, it's always been her ambition to revitalise the crop and to produce her own Paradise cocoa beans one day. That's why they employed an estate manager last year to oversee the plantation.'

'You mean Zach? That handsome hunk who's taken the guys out on a rainforest scavenger hunt today?'

'Actually, no. I meant his colleague, Jake Lawson,' laughed Millie, her stomach performing a swift somersault at the mention of Zach's name. 'Zach manages Claudia's Cotswolds estate where she runs her UK cookery school. He did a swap so that Jake could go back home for a few months whilst his mother receives treatment for cancer.'

A sudden splat of rain landed on the wooden planks in front of Millie and Imogen, followed swiftly by several more.

'Oh, my God! Is it raining?'

'The locals call it liquid sunshine,' said Millie, smiling at the bride-to-be's wrinkled nose and upturned lip at the brief absence of the sun. 'Without the daily deluge, we wouldn't be feasting our eyes on all this tropical magnificence! Don't worry. It's just a shower, usual service will resume shortly.'

'This isn't a shower, it's a monsoon!' tutted Julia, dashing past them to shelter in the kitchen as the rain continued to hammer down with vicious acrimony. 'Would you like us to help you tidy up the kitchen?'

'No, thank you!' exclaimed Ella, in a tone that brooked no argument.

'It's very kind of you to offer, though,' said Millie, who privately would have loved to have taken Julia up on her offer. 'See you tomorrow – is a ten o'clock start okay?'

'Perfect.'

Chapter Two

Millie waved the women off in their hire car, a gleaming white Mercedes SUV, before turning to hug Ella. She took a few moments to enjoy the unfamiliar surge of confidence and accomplishment that whipped through her body. If someone had told her two weeks ago that she would be presenting a cookery school in the tropical island paradise of St Lucia she would have told them they were delusional. She couldn't wait to call her sister to reiterate her heartfelt thanks for recommending her services to Claudia when Jen had been unable to help, and to share every single detail of the day's events with her.

'That was one of the most amazing days of my life!' she sighed, her heart ballooning with pride at what they had managed to pull off against all the odds. 'Everything went without a hitch – unless you count those exploding chocolate eggs Gracie insisted on daubing with edible glitter and daisy-shaped rice paper flowers!'

'I agree – it's been absolutely fantastic,' smiled Ella as she filled a blue plastic bucket with hot water and added a generous spritz of disinfectant. 'You're a natural behind the lectern, Millie. But the day isn't over yet. I reckon there's a good hour of clearing up to do!'

Millie surveyed the chaos in the kitchen. She cringed when she realised that most of the culinary debris was hers. Not only was the marble top of the demonstration workstation dusted in a light coating of cocoa powder interspersed with slivers of red chillies, but there were mixing bowls, measuring jugs and wooden spoons stuffed into the sink awaiting a twirl in the dishwasher, not to mention the discarded aprons and tea towels draped on the bar stools. The copper jam pan she had used to make the marmalade had toppled onto its side and spilled its contents onto the bench – the whole place looked like Marmalade Armageddon.

Working in the choreographed unison gained from spending two weeks together in the tiny kitchen above the villa's garage where Millie had her temporary home, the tidying up part of the day was finished in no time. Millie yanked off her Marigolds, draped them over the swan-necked tap, and reached for the pretty glass pitcher to prepare a jug of home-made lemonade from the lemons grown just outside the kitchen window.

'Shall we take this out to the veranda?'

'Great idea. I could do with a sit down! I've enjoyed every minute of the course, but it's hard on the old feet, isn't it?'

Millie glanced down at the kitten heels Ella had customised with gold and silver sequins and smiled. Maybe tomorrow her co-presenter would reconsider her suggestion she choose a pair of ballet flats – or maybe not. Ella loved fashion, the more flamboyant and colourful the better.

They settled in a pair of white rattan chairs, resting their tired feet on the plump cushions, sipping their tangy lemonade and taking the time to enjoy the view. Millie knew she would never grow tired of drinking in its magnificence. In the foreground, just beyond the balcony where they relaxed, was the most stunning expanse of translucent aquamarine. The infinity pool's decking had been embellished with six navy-and-white striped sun-loungers and was bordered by a necklace of lush cocoa trees, their leaves sporting a glossy sheen from the recent downpour. But she barely noticed this tropical splendour compared to the majesty of the wider panorama.

To her left, at the foot of Gros Piton and Petit Piton nestled the old French capital of St Lucia, Soufrière, its church spire and telegraph poles jutting from a patchwork of red-roofed homes stitched together by swaying palm trees. This was Millie's idea of paradise and Claudia had certainly selected the most appropriate title for her new venture in the Caribbean. The last vestiges of nervous tension she had harboured in the pit of her stomach all day melted away and she allowed a satisfied sigh to escape her lips.

'What time is Henri coming to collect you?'

Ella checked her watch, a gem-encrusted masterpiece that wouldn't have looked out of place on the most bling-addicted celebrity, but it matched her personality perfectly.

'Around six – after he's "put the paper to bed"!'

Ella chuckled at the expression, a rich belly rumble that filled Millie with affection for the woman who had welcomed her into her life and nurtured not only her culinary skills, but also her emotional wellbeing. She thought back to the day she arrived on St Lucia, right in the middle of the daily deluge, clutching her trusty scrap box filled with the recipes she had collected over the years scribbled on till receipts and beer mats, wondering why she hadn't insisted on sticking to her plan to spend the holiday with her mother at her childhood home in the South of France.

But then she had met Ella, and they had spent an amazing two weeks triple-testing every recipe on the Chocolate & Confetti course, whisking meringues, slicing mangoes, peeling cassava, scooping out passion fruit and grating nutmeg. However, the icing on the cake had been their easy camaraderie. They had laughed and giggled as they worked, sharing increasingly intimate details of their lives, their loves, and their dreams for the future.

'I wonder how Lottie has survived her first day in charge of the Purple Parrot?' Millie mused. 'I know Dylan and Travis offered to help her out, but I bet she's been run off her feet.'

'Like you, Millie, Lottie is an extremely capable and resourceful young woman. In fact, I'm sure she'll have that bar ship-shape and running like clockwork in no time.'

Millie's heart softened when she conjured up an image of her friend Lottie, a gap-year lingerer who had fallen in love with the Caribbean vibe as well as a certain surfer dude by the name of Dylan who owned the local diving school. She had spent months admiring him from the veranda of the bar-cum-restaurant where she had worked as a waitress until its proprietor had been arrested for smuggling cocaine using hollowed out cocoa pods he'd stolen from Claudia's plantation. Either Lottie pinned on the badge of temporary manager or the Purple Parrot would have been forced to close its doors and she would have lost her job.

Proving the age-old adage that every cloud had a silver lining, after Andrew's apprehension Lottie and Dylan had realised that they were perfect for each other and Millie didn't think Lottie had stopped smiling since! She was prepared to bet her last bottle of rum that the two of them, along with their friend and local artist Travis, had pulled together to keep regulars and tourists alike supplied with a plethora of delicious, freshly cooked Caribbean seafood and a never-ending supply of the Purple Parrot's signature cocktails – although she assumed Lottie would have renamed the eponymous Andy's Blast whilst its namesake languished in the town's police station awaiting news of his fate.

'Has Henri heard anything about what'll happen to Andrew through his contacts at the *Soufrière Tribune*?'

'When I spoke to him at lunchtime he was complaining about Leon's refusal to divulge even the smallest detail of their investigations to the press. But you know my son, Millie, he's nothing if not tenacious – and the scourge of the Caribbean drug trade and the criminals who peddle its misery have become something of a specialised subject for him since he joined the paper. I suspect he'll have spent the whole afternoon pestering anyone and everyone for even a snippet of information to splash across the headlines. Would you like a lift down to Soufrière with us? Or do you have a more intimate evening planned?'

Millie couldn't fail to catch the glint of mischief in Ella eyes and she knew immediately what she was alluding to. A plethora of emotions jangled around her body and for a moment she was unable to elucidate her feelings coherently.

On the one hand, she could think of nothing better than waving Ella off in Henri's rust bucket of a Fiat before sprinting over to Zach's lodge in the rainforest for an evening of sparkling banter rounded off with several kisses under the stars as he walked her back to her studio. She adored his company and the way he made her feel as though she could accomplish anything she put her mind to. His unassailable confidence in her had worked its magic and she was bursting to relay how successful the very first Paradise Cookery School had been and to thank him for his part in that.

And, of course, she couldn't forget the way her body reacted when his dark mahogany eyes, edged with the longest lashes she had seen on a man, held hers – she positively zinged with desire!

However, on the other hand, she had no idea how Zach felt about her and that scared her. She had thought Luke had loved her. Hadn't they been about to celebrate their engagement with their family and friends at a lavish party before he dropped the bombshell that he'd been seeing someone else? And did she really want a holiday fling? Whilst there was nothing wrong with that, if she were honest with herself, she knew that where Zach was concerned she would want much more than that. Would they really be able to continue seeing each other when they were both back in the UK, bearing in mind the distance between London and the Cotswolds and the demands of their respective careers? Could she cope with renewed feelings of loss? Could she really do that to herself?

Confusion reigned and she had no answers that would help erase the obstacles to a relationship with Zach. Ella had seen her hesitation and reached across the table to pat her hand.

'Millie, dear, you look like you've lost a dollar and found a penny! Relax! Have some fun – you deserve it after how hard you've worked today. It's obvious to even the most unobservant onlooker that you and Zach have a great deal of chemistry going on. You know, we have to snatch every opportunity life tosses in our path because none of us know what might be waiting for us around the corner!'

Millie met Ella's eyes and saw the briefest wisp of sadness floating in their depths. The proud tilt of her chin belied the vagaries of a life lived as a lone parent prepared to do whatever was necessary to make a better life for her son. She knew her friend's story and whilst it was a sad one, Ella had never entertained even a smidgeon of self-pity. She had truly loved Henri's father, Jean-Pierre, another gap-year rambler who had been seduced by the island's laid-back lifestyle, exuberant friendliness, and casual acceptance of life's bounty – until Ella had discovered she was pregnant and he'd hot-footed it back to Paris. Her friend hadn't seen him since.

'Ah, here's my Henri!'

Millie smiled as she heard the high-pitched whine of the Fiat's tiny engine straining to make it up the steep slope leading to the courtyard at the rear of the villa. Following in Ella's fragrant slipstream, she grabbed the huge Tupperware box filled with baked goodies Ella intended to share with Henri and her best friend, Denise.

'Hi, Henri!'

Millie leaned into the car and deposited kisses on his cheeks, inhaling the spicy aroma of his cologne. There was no doubt about it, Ella's son was an extremely handsome guy. With a strong jaw sporting a trendy smattering of stubble and dark ebony eyes oozing intelligence, he could have easily landed a starring role in a Caribbean romcom instead of working long hours as an intrepid journalist – not an easy job when the majority of his stories featured a side order of drug-infused violence.

'Hey, Millie. From the smiles on your faces, I take it the inaugural Paradise Cookery School course went well?'

'Of course it did, darling!' declared Ella, squeezing her bulk into the front passenger seat and accepting the Tupperware box from Millie, placing it carefully on her lap. 'But what I want to know is if there's any more news on the cocoa pod fiasco? Has Andrew been charged?'

'Investigations are ongoing,' parroted Henri, rolling his eyes in irritation at the lack of progress.

'Good! I hope Andrew gets what he deserves. It was a despicable thing to do to Claudia and Tim. Okay, see you tomorrow, Millie, bright and early.'

Millie stood in the courtyard, waving off her friend, watching the little car scoot down the hill like an out-of-control roller skate until the red tail lights disappeared around the corner. Dusk tickled the far horizon sending tendrils of apricot and salmon-pink across the sky and the silhouettes of the Pitons grew dark against the silver grey of the sea. A pandemonium of parrots flitted from cocoa tree to palm tree to banana tree searching for a comfortable perch upon which to rest for the night whilst the sun-baked earth filled the air with a delicate floral scent.

As Millie climbed the stairs to her studio, a wave of exhaustion descended over her, dragging her bones southwards and causing her eyelids to droop. She decided that the best thing to do would be to take a shower and treat herself to an early night. She was excited about the next day's itinerary and was keen to ensure it too went according to plan, especially as she now hoped that her dream to become a cookery school presenter when she returned home could actually become a reality.

Chapter Three

'Hi, everyone. Welcome back to the Paradise Cookery School!' said Millie as she concertina-ed back the full-width French doors to allow the scant morning breeze into the kitchen.

'Hi, Millie. Hi, Ella,' chorused the enthusiastic bakers as they grabbed a freshly laundered apron each and made their way to their respective work-stations.

'I'm sorry, Millie, Mum can't make it today,' smirked Imogen, catching her sister's eye. 'She sends her apologies.'

'So she should!' laughed Karen. 'I've never seen her as sozzled as she was last night.'

'Yes, but don't you think it's romantic?'

'Everything's *romantic* to you at the moment, Immie. Anyway, it's probably just a holiday fling.'

'It might not be,' interrupted Carla, tying her pale-lemon apron securely and slumping down on a bar stool, not looking exactly daisy-fresh herself.

Millie's ears pricked up with interest. She loved engaging in a bit of harmless gossip and without her best friend Poppy around she had been starved of her regular fix. However, she was reluctant to intrude on family chatter that was none of her business. Fortunately, Karen wasn't as circumspect with her mother's privacy.

'Would you believe that Mum bumped into an old flame in the hotel bar last night? Apparently, she and this guy called Brad Maxwell went to art school together – they even dated for a couple of months before they graduated. I remember Mum telling me about him the Christmas after Dad died when we were going through a box of old photographs. Brad left to take up an internship at a New York art gallery and asked Mum to go with him but she'd just been offered a job as a trainee interior designer at Liberty and their relationship sort of fizzled out because of the distance. Then she met Dad and, as the saying goes, the rest is history.'

'He is kind of dreamy though, don't you think?' said Imogen, her chin cupped in her hand. 'Sort of an older George Clooney. Mum's definitely got excellent taste.'

'Well, looking at their body language last night, they could have melted a chocolate bar at ten paces!' grinned Harriet, as she gathered her copper-coloured hair up from her shoulders and tied it into a high ponytail.

'Yes, well, she should be here instead of lolling around the pool nursing her headache,' tutted Karen, clearly upset about her mother rekindling the friendship.

'Well, she did promise to chase up the flowers with the wedding planner, didn't she? And the personalised confetti. You know, Kaz, I'm started to think Mum's right about her. She's definitely been conspicuous by her absence since we arrived. Don't get me wrong, I'm not as obsessed as Mum is about all the arrangements, but I would like to have a wedding bouquet and a couple of posies for my lovely bridesmaids and flower girl!'

'Heaven help the woman if Julia finds out she's forgotten to organise the butterflies!' laughed Carla. 'Maybe we'll be able to round up a flotilla of turtle doves for you instead, Immie.'

'I'm pleased Mum has reconnected with an old friend. She deserves a bit of romance after everything she's been through. Dad's been gone for three years now and she's refused to even think about having dinner with anyone. She's only forty-eight. I don't want to think of her being alone for the rest of her life. I wonder if she'll invite him as her plus one to the wedding?'

'Immie! It was a drink, that's all.'

'And a walk round the grounds in the moon-light.'

'Ah, she didn't tell me that bit.'

'Well, that's probably because—'

'Okay!' interrupted Ella before the sisters embarked on a sibling squabble. 'A very warm welcome to the second day of your Chocolate and Confetti course here at the Paradise Cookery School. Today we're going to be showing you how to create a new twist on a Mississippi mud pie, experiment with a chocolate shortbread recipe my grandmother invented, and prepare a pina colada trifle made with chocolate custard and laced with Caribbean rum. So ladies, aprons on, let's get started.'

All the women, apart from Gracie, who wore her pink glittery sandshoes with pride, had clearly learned a lesson from the previous day and had swapped their designer heels for embellished flip-flops or, in the case of Carla, neon-coloured Skechers. They watched in fascinated silence as Ella talked them through her family recipe, liberally interspersed with anecdotes about her childhood in St Lucia. Then it was over to them and, like the previous day, the burble of contented conversation accompanied the occasional burst of laughter as the students crafted their own, individual versions of the recipes.

Before they knew it, lunchtime arrived. Ella lit the barbeque on the veranda and set about grilling red snapper marinated in lime juice and diced chillies, tuna and chicken skewers coated in fresh mango salsa, and for dessert, bananas with their skins sliced open and stuffed with cubes of pineapple drizzled with honey. The aroma of char-grilled meat and fish wafted through the air as the party tucked in with gusto.

'I love your earrings, Imogen. I've never seen anything like them.'

Ella was something of an aficionado of eclectic jewellery items and always sported a vast array of bold pieces, most of which had been hand-crafted by her friend Anisha, who had a shop in Soufrière. However, Millie had to agree with her. Imogen's earrings-and-necklace combo was exquisite. The twisted silver links caught the midday sun, streaming through the French windows into the Paradise Cookery School's kitchen, beautifully.

'Thank you! I'm so pleased you said that,' Imogen beamed. 'These are from a brand-new range I designed myself especially for the bridal party, but after the wedding, I plan to roll them out to my clients.'

'Ah, so you're a jewellery designer?'

'Yes, I trained as a silversmith. I mainly do commissions, but I've always wanted to move into the wider bridal jewellery market. Everything went manic when Pippa Middleton was photographed wearing one of my pieces at Wimbledon in July and now I can't keep up with demand. It's amazing and I'm so excited about the future. I've made our wedding rings, too.'

Millie's heart softened at the excitement written across Imogen's face when she spoke of her impending nuptials. She really did look like the happiest girl on the island, with a smattering of freckles on her upturned nose, and her hair smoothed down into an elegant chignon to combat the attack of frizz that was inevitable in the humidity of the Caribbean. Despite the fact that her mother had turned her wedding into a royal occasion, Imogen seemed to have taken it in good spirits. And why shouldn't she? Millie had taken a quick peek at the website of the wedding venue. How could anyone complain about getting married in a magnificent white gazebo amid the lush mani-cured gardens of an upmarket St Lucian hotel?

'Shall we get back to the kitchen?' asked Ella, replenishing everyone's glasses with home-made iced lemonade for them to take back to their benches.

'What's on the itinerary for this afternoon?' asked Harriet, dabbing her lips with a napkin after her second helping of chocolate trifle and snatching up a white chocolate chip cookie to take back to her workstation with her.

'Millie's going to showcase her fabulous chocolate and orange lava fondants and then I'll guide you through the most delectable chocolate tiramisu bombe – and you've guessed it – it'll be soaked in Caribbean rum.'

The women set to work. The all-encompassing fragrance of warm cocoa and melted orange caramel was so intoxicating Millie wished someone would bottle it so she could feast her senses on it whenever she wanted. It would be instant happiness in a jar!

'What did you say the guys were up to today?' asked Karen.

'I think Alex said it was scuba diving this morning and then a quad bike safari this afternoon.'

'No offence, Millie, because I've had an absolute ball learning about all these chocolate-based goodies, not to mention the tasting sessions,' said Carla, tucking the sides of her short bob behind her ears before reaching for her beloved camera to take a few snaps of her creations to post on Instagram. 'But I would have loved to join in with the guys this afternoon for a race around the plantation on quad bikes.'

'What? Even in the rain?' laughed Millie, glancing through the window as the heavens opened to deliver the daily deluge of liquid sunshine. She didn't think it was wise to go on to say that she couldn't think of anything she would rather not do than spent the afternoon on one of the over-grown mechanical bluebottles Zach loved.

'When do you think the boys will get here?' asked Imogen, clearly keen to be reunited with Alex as soon as possible.

Millie checked the little silver watch that had belonged to her French grandmother. 'It's three-thirty, so probably in about half an hour or so. Zach said to expect them around four o'clock.'

'Well, if my super-organised boyfriend has anything to do with it they'll be here on the dot – and with him in the lead of course!' muttered Carla, taking her camera over to the patio doors and pointing the lens at the palm trees surrounding the swimming pool, their trunks leaning almost horizontally to the weather's torment. 'It was Greg's idea to put up the ribbon across the courtyard as a finishing line, and he's even asked me to take a picture of everyone as they arrive just in case there's a photo-finish.'

'Well, if you don't mind, I'll give that delightful experience a miss. I'd like to get Gracie back to the hotel for a nap before we go out for dinner tonight,' said Karen. 'I've never been a fan of watching grown men compete for the Testosterone Trophy.'

'You really just want to subject Mum to an intensive interrogation about the suitability of Brad as an escort, don't you?' laughed Imogen, coiling her arm around her sister's waist and ruffling her niece's blonde ringlets that had morphed into a halo of candyfloss.

'Too right! One of us has to look out for her. We don't want strange men taking advantage of her good nature, do we?'

'She's a grown woman, Karen, and she deserves a bit of fun. Leave her be and let her enjoy her sojourn in the sun.'

Karen leaned in to kiss her sister on the cheek before dashing with Gracie to their hire car and disappearing through the curtain of rain down the steep incline towards the town at the bottom of the hill.

Imogen and her two bridesmaids took their time preparing extra-strength cocktails from the recipe cards designed by Lottie and when the rain stopped, they took them out to the veranda so that Millie and Ella could make a start on the tidying up. Millie had to confess that Tuesday's culinary clutter was even worse than the day before. Every counter top and cupboard door had a generous splodge of melted chocolate smeared across its surface and the whole kitchen looked like a chocolate firework had exploded.

'Hey! Is that them?' cried Imogen, unfolding her long legs and leading the race to the courtyard at the front of the villa.

It was exactly the excuse Millie needed to ditch the cleaning and welcome the men back from their afternoon's exploits. As they waited on the steps, the unmistakable buzz of a quad bike's engine pierced through the air from deep within the thick, jungle-like vegetation on the eastern border of the Croft cocoa plantation. Millie shielded her eyes with her hand and concentrated on the spot at the far end of the driveway where a row of palm trees stood to attention like a battalion of sentries.

'I reckon it'll be Alex out in front!'

'Not if Greg has anything to do with it,' said Carla, coiling the strap of her Pentax around her index finger. 'You know how competitive he is. He'd even try to out-race Lewis Hamilton!'

'Well, it definitely won't be Owen,' murmured Harriet, her face flooded with concern for her husband. 'He was horrified when Alex suggested this trek as part of his stag week itinerary – I don't know how Greg managed to talk him into it. He had fun on the rainforest treasure hunt yesterday, though, and he's excited about the fishing trip that Dylan from the Dive Shack has organised for tomorrow, but anything to do with four wheels makes him really apprehensive, especially on these roads. Have you seen the potholes! I've seen smaller swimming pools!'

Millie cast a covert glance in Imogen's direction. Earlier on that afternoon the bride-to-be had confided the reason Harriet was constantly glancing at her mobile phone, her expression wreathed in anxiety, and why Owen shied away from getting behind a wheel more than was absolutely necessary. If she were in Harriet's position, she would be exactly the same and her heart gave a nip of sympathy.

'Yay! It's Alex!' squealed Imogen, bouncing up and down on the spot, clapping her hands in jubilation as the frontrunner emerged from the arboreal sanctuary and shot up the driveway towards the official finishing line.

Imogen was right, her fiancé *was* in the lead, but only by a few seconds as Greg appeared from a different gap in the trees fifty metres to their left, his head bent low over the handlebars, revving the engine and expelling a cloud of exhaust fumes as he tried to coax the last ounce of speed from the rusty mechanical beast.

A blast of excitement erupted in Millie's chest when she saw that Zach was in third place. It was all she could do to prevent herself from coming over all Eliza Doolittle-esque as she joined the chorus to encourage her preferred winner.

'Alex!' yelled Imogen, cupping her hands around her lips and screaming '*Go Alex!*' in a very unladylike fashion before linking her arms through Millie's and Harriet's. 'Come on, ladies. Let's get over to the finishing line. Come on, Carla. It looks like we might need that photo-finish after all!'

The high-pitched squeal of the engines was getting louder and the waft of diesel fumes invaded Millie's nostrils as she watched the string of quad bikes buck and bounce along the road like a procession of kangaroos on steroids. She wasn't a fan of the quad bikes Zach loved so much. She glanced around the gathering in the courtyard then longingly towards the kitchen where she knew Ella was busy tidying up from their Chocolate & Confetti session. She knew where she would rather be, even if it meant doing the washing up.

She intended to offer the guys a cool beer before they were whisked off by Greg for the next part of their itinerary – an evening of bar-based activities in Soufrière. However, she knew that no delay in his meticulous scheduling would be tolerated for the whimsy of food preparation and consumption. Someone perhaps needed to remind Greg, a former sergeant in the Royal Marines, that the pre-wedding celebrations were not one of his military field manoeuvres. And she'd thought Zach was obsessive!

'Oh, thank God! There's Owen – bringing up the rear as usual!' Harriet sighed and Millie saw the relief flood the young girl's attractive features. 'I thought he might have fallen off or something…'

Millie, Imogen and Harriet loitered at the red ribbon Greg had insisted they rigged up for the victor to drive through, whilst Carla crouched down onto her haunches next to the wooden post and levelled her camera lens, poised to snap a picture of the winner's triumph.

'Yay! Alex! You won!' screeched Imogen, her chignon bouncing around her cheeks, as she rushed forward to hug her bridegroom-to-be before raising herself up onto her tiptoes to kiss him tenderly on the lips, her adoration lighting up her face. 'Well done, Greg! You were awesome, too!'

Only a couple of seconds had separated Alex from his best man, but that was all that was needed. A wide grin split his face as he yanked off his safety helmet and strode over to offer Greg his palm in commiseration.

'Great ride, Greg! That was a truly exhilarating experience. I might even be forced to reconsider my earlier criticism of the over-the-top schedule for my stag week. You've definitely delivered a fantastic programme of activities so far!'

'Hey, Zach, well done to you, too – third place in this troop of ex-military competitors is a fantastic achievement!' laughed Imogen, striding forward to give him a quick congratulatory peck on the cheek, sending a mischievous glance in Millie's direction, clearly aware of the spark of electricity that flowed between them. 'Ooops, sorry, Millie!'

Millie smiled at Imogen's teasing, enjoying the sensation of being an integral part of the welcoming committee, not to mention the way Zach had raised his perfectly sculpted eyebrows and smirked at Imogen's blatant assumption they were a couple.

Her thoughts spun back to the day she had met Zach Barker. Initially, they had irritated the skin off each other due to the fact they possessed character traits at opposite ends of the organisational spectrum. However, over the subsequent two weeks their tolerance of each other's foibles had ballooned while they worked to achieve the impossible – getting a group of laid-back Caribbean workmen to pull out all the stops and complete the villa's kitchen renovations in time for Imogen and her friends' arrival.

Due to their constant squabbling, their friendship had surprised her, but her blossoming relationship with him had been responsible for papering over the cracks in her heart after her unceremonious abandonment only six months ago. With Zach's help, she had succeeded in grappling with her sorrow, and had discarded the mantle of gloom she had habitually draped around her shoulders as some sort of protective battle armour after her break-up with Luke. Zach had called her out and she had risen to the challenge of putting the past behind her. She now woke each morning with a smile on her face, confident that she had a better-than-average chance that the struggle to bedtime would be devoid of melancholy.

'Come on, Owen! Put some welly into it!' called Greg, waving his arms in encouragement.

The whole crowd turned in unison to watch Owen, his face a curious shade of overworked putty, as he covered the final hundred yards to the finishing line. Harriet rushed forward to pick up the ribbon so he could drive through it like a conquering hero. With only fifty yards to go, Owen raised his hand in a triumphant fist pump to acknowledge the group, but mainly to indicate to the First Assistant Director in charge of his personal horror show that he had succeeded. However, in that split second of distraction, he lost control of his quad bike. The handlebars swung to his left and he headed at speed towards Millie.

'Agh! Millie, look out!' screamed Imogen.

Millie found she was frozen to the spot as she watched on in terror whilst Owen and his rampaging quad bike bore down on her at speed. She screwed her eyes shut and prepared herself for the inevitable impact and the ensuing pain. Before she knew what was happening, she was flying through the air and landing with a thump in an adjacent ditch.

The shock of the collision hit her like a sledge-hammer to the solar plexus. A dry retch escaped from her throat, yet there was none of the expected agony because she had experienced a surprisingly soft landing. She slowly explored each one of her senses in turn and found she was no worse for her unexpected brush with serious injury. Then she glanced down to see a pair of arms secured around her chest.

'Maddening Millie strikes again!' Zach groaned in her ear as a waft of his familiar citrusy cologne invaded her nostrils. 'Do you think you could climb off me so I can breathe again? I swear you've put on weight since the last time I rescued you from certain death. If you're going to make a habit of this, the least you can do is cut down on the chocolate brownies!'

Millie was about to shoot back an equally caustic comment, but reconsidered when she remembered the position she was in.

'Sorry, sorry. And, erm, thanks, Zach. For saving me.'

'The best way you can thank me is by working on your tendency to cause turmoil wherever you go. A man can get seriously injured being around you. I think I need to call my broker and increase my life insurance cover.'

Zach uncoiled his arms from around her chest and turned to face her. His black T-shirt was drenched from his brief dalliance at the bottom of the post-monsoon gulley and it clung to his torso, highlighting his taut stomach muscles, and his neatly gelled mahogany hair was dotted with dry leaves and blades of grass. Even in his dishevelled state, he oozed brooding good looks and a curl of attraction twisted through Millie's veins. His lips were mere inches from hers, his breath tickling her earlobe, but she concluded that, sadly, it was probably not the right moment to indulge in a repeat performance of their previous kissing marathon.

Zach leaped to his feet and offered Millie his palm to pull her upright, his eyes dancing with mischief.

'You could just come over and say hello? Maybe a peck on the cheek like Imogen opted for? But, oh no. Nothing so mundane for Amelia Harper where excitement and surprise are the buzz-words of the day.'

Millie was saved from delivering her rant of retaliation by the arrival of Imogen and Alex.

'Oh my God! Millie, are you hurt?'

'I'm fine...'

'Whilst I, on the other hand, have suffered the indignity of being splattered from head to toe with Caribbean mud!' smirked Zach, just about able to conceal his laughter at the comical situation he found himself in. 'It's just as well Ella's already informed me how beneficial it is for a blemish-free complexion!'

'Not that you need it!' laughed Harriet, turning to survey Millie, the relief that all was well scrawled across her features. 'Owen, why don't you give them both a quick once over? You *are* a doctor!'

'Not any more,' he murmured before meeting Millie's eyes. 'Millie, Zach, I'm so, so sorry! Can you forgive me? It's all my fault. I got over-confident. I should have known what would happen, what always happens whenever I…'

'It's okay, Owen. Don't worry about it. We're both fine. No harm done.'

'Greg Collins, don't you *ever* ask Owen to do anything like that again!' demanded Harriet. 'This is supposed to be a fun-filled week for everyone. You are one of the hardest task-masters I've ever come across and that includes those physio guys Owen had to deal with at the rehab centre! I shouldn't have to remind you that none of you are in the forces anymore.'

Greg had the decency to fix an expression of contrition on his handsome face. Clearly, he accepted the accusation that his carefully crafted schedule of activities had pushed Owen beyond his comfort zone.

'Sorry, Harriet. Apologies, Owen. And to you, Immie and Alex. I promise I'll tone down the heroics from now on.'

'Good, because before Harriet even has the chance to draw her sword, Mum will kill you with her bare hands if any of the wedding photographs are marred by one of the gang sporting a plaster cast!' warned Imogen.

Greg visibly shuddered. 'Gosh, please don't threaten me with Julia's wrath!'

The group laughed and the tension that had been building since the men's arrival on the scene evaporated. Millie surreptitiously brushed the vegetation from her shins and made a bee-line for the kitchen where Ella, who had thankfully been oblivious to the drama unfolding in the courtyard, handed round cool beers and iced tea.

'Another eventful day in the life of Manic Millie!' teased Zach, snaking his arm around Millie's shoulders as he supped his beer. 'What am I going to do for excitement around here when you leave us next week?'

Chapter Four

An hour later, Ella and Millie waved goodbye to the wedding party, all of whom were in high spirits. Everyone had enjoyed their chosen activities that day and the conversation had been animated, with Alex and Greg vying for bragging rights for the best quad bike rider, causing Imogen and Carla to roll their eyes in amusement.

Zach offered to give Ella a lift down the hill to Soufrière where she intended to meet up with Henri for dinner, and at last Millie was alone. She slipped off her shoes, grabbed a beer, and went to sit on the edge of the pool, her toes floating in the cool water. Darkness had fallen but the atmosphere was still humid. All around her, the eternal soundtrack of the tropical rainforest chirped and squawked and scuttled as the nocturnal animals went about their business. She tipped her head back and inhaled the exotic perfume of the fallen lemons, crushed underfoot, mingled with jasmine and something altogether earthier.

A wave of contentment rippled through her body as she appreciated her good fortune at being in such an idyllic place, doing what she loved most with people who were happy to be there. Never in her wildest dreams had she thought she would ever find herself relaxing by a Caribbean pool, thanking the director of her fate for her blessings, and yet, here she was.

Suddenly, she wanted to share her good fortune with someone, so instead of retiring early for the night like she did yesterday, she decided to take a walk to the wooden lodge at the other side of the cocoa plantation that Zach called home. She checked her watch. He should be back from dropping Ella off by now. She collected her shoes, grabbed a bottle of red wine and a torch, and made her way along the path that wound through the cocoa palms from the villa to the cabin.

As Millie drew closer to the lodge, the ambient calm of the night was rudely interrupted by the buzz of a chain saw. She slowed her pace, not wanting to alarm Zach by her approach and cause an accident, until she came to a stop just beyond the clearing where his temporary home was located. Amber light flooded the area where Zach was busy working, the chain saw sending chips of wood and sawdust into the air like confetti at a wedding. She saw that he was working on sculpting a thick tree trunk into a sort of rustic bench. He worked in a controlled and precise manner, pausing to flick up the visor of his safety helmet to check his progress before resuming his careful carving.

The whine of the saw stopped again. She watched Zach reach for a bottle of water and empty the contents into his mouth, his Adam's apple bobbing rhythmically at his throat as he gulped down the drink. For the first time, Millie noticed he had removed his shirt and a spasm of desire shot into her chest and travelled southwards. Zach wiped his lips with the back of his hand, sending droplets of water onto his naked chest where they glistened in the golden light. The well-defined muscles on his abdomen contracted as he continued with his woodcutting and Millie suddenly felt as though she had downed the bottle of red wine she was still clutching in one go!

She recognised physical attraction when she experienced it. A hot ember of lust had ignited in what she had thought was a dormant part of her body and she wanted to stay in that precise spot for the rest of the evening, relishing the intoxicating sight before her eyes. She didn't want to invade Zach's privacy, but she was unsure how to make herself known without making it look like she was some kind of voyeur. Warmth flooded her cheeks, but it was the heat of attraction that was travelling around her veins that worried her. In the end, the decision was taken out of her hands.

'Woof!'

Her cover was blown. She glanced at Zach and his gaze connected with hers, a slow smile turning his lips upwards into the familiar smirk.

'Looks like we have a visitor, Binks.'

Millie bent down to fondle the black-and-white spaniel's silky ears to give herself time to calm her rampaging emotions and hope that the colour in her cheeks faded before she had to face Zach. Perspiration collected on her temples and beneath her breasts, and she craved a mouthful of the water Zach had been drinking earlier. A pair of steel-capped work boots appeared and she slowly raised herself from her haunches to meet his eyes.

'Sorry, I didn't want to disturb you whilst you were… were working.'

She realised that Zach was standing only inches away from her and she could feel his breath, coming in spurts from his recent exertion, on her cheek. Clearly he had seen how flustered she was to find him outside the log cabin in little more than a pair of figure-hugging shorts and was enjoying her discomfort, so to make matters worse he took a step closer.

'How long have you been standing here?' murmured Zach, his voice as low and smooth as a caress, his eyes flicking down to her lips then back to her eyes.

'Erm, not long. I just… I just thought we could share a bottle of…'

Zach was now millimetres away from her. The electricity in the space between them was almost too much to bear and Millie was finding it hard to breathe. She raised the bottle of wine to show Zach what she meant but the sudden movement caused her to lose her footing and she tumbled backwards into one of the magnolia bushes that framed the wooden cabin, ending up spread-eagled amongst the leaves and unable to extricate herself without his assistance.

'Oh my God!' howled Zach, his eyes widened with mirth. 'Mishap Millie strikes again! Well, I suppose you're nothing if not consistent.'

'Are you just going to stand there laughing, or are you going to help me out of here?'

'What do you think, Binks? Should we be chivalrous and help the young lady out of her embarrassing predicament or, and this is my preferred option, should I rush to the cabin for my mobile phone and upload this photographic gem to my Instagram account?'

'Very funny!'

The cute dimples that bracketed Zach's mouth reappeared as he offered Millie his hand to drag her free of the tree's embrace. To her horror, he then began to brush away the leaves that clung to her T-shirt and capri pants, spending an inordinate amount of time on the arboreal debris that had attached itself to her bottom.

'Erm...'

'Just let me...' Zach reached forward, his thumb and forefinger extended towards her curls, which had now expanded into an unattractive halo of blonde frizz. 'You have a bit of...'

Millie knew that if she leaned forward just another inch her lips would connect with Zach's. Go for it! screamed her heart, but before her brain could reconnect to her modem and react to the order, Zach had disentangled the dried palm frond and called Binks to heel.

'Fancy a spag bol to go with that wine?' Zach called over his shoulder as if nothing had happened.

'You're offering to cook?'

'Well, there's no way I'm letting you loose in my kitchen, that's for sure. Don't forget I've seen what devastation you can wreak in a kitchen! I don't think Binks could cope with the cleaning up. The invitation is only valid if you promise *not* to interfere – physically or verbally.'

'Deal.'

'Come on then.'

Zach led the way up the wooden steps and through the front door of the lodge. He settled an excited Binks in his tartan-lined basket with a reassuring pat and a dog biscuit from his pocket and crossed the open-plan lounge area to the kitchen

'Grab a seat and I'll pour the wine.'

'Oh, I can help with that.'

'No, thank you! Remember your promise?'

However, Millie had already opened one of the kitchen cupboards to search for a couple of glasses. Even her sister Jen, who was the Queen of Culinary Orderliness, didn't organise her kitchen cupboards with such meticulous attention to detail. She wasn't surprised to see an array of jars of varying exoticness – Caribbean spices, dried herbs, flavoured salts – every label lined up in military precision.

'I can't believe you store your spices in alphabetical order!'

Zach gently removed the jar of dried oregano from her hand, returned it to its rightful place, and shooed her away to the lounge.

'Go and keep Binks company.'

Whilst Zach assembled the dinner ingredients and set two places at the pine table, Millie took the opportunity to survey the décor. Like the kitchen, the room was meticulously tidy. A carved mahogany mask presided over the redundant fireplace like a painted witch doctor ready to cast a spell. There was a hand-made bookcase next to the door that Millie assumed led to the bedroom, and she had to quickly squash the image of Zach sprawled out on his bed asleep, naked but for a cotton sheet.

She decided to investigate the bookcase's contents, curious to know what type of books Zach liked to read. *Tropical Caribbean Birds*? *Quad Bikes and how to Race Them*? *Fifty Shades of Grey*, maybe? Millie couldn't prevent a gasp of interest escaping her lips.

'What?' asked Zach from the breakfast bar where he was slicing onions with the precision of a master craftsman before weighing out the pasta on a set of digital scales. One of Claudia's cookery books was propped open on the bench.

'Oh, nothing. You know, this really is a very luxuriously appointed lodge.'

'I have Jake to thank for that. He's lived here for the last two years and you're right, he's certainly put a very comfortable stamp on what could have been a much more rustic abode.'

'What sort of place do you have back in the UK?'

'I live in the lodge at the entrance to Claudia and Tim's manor house in a little village called Berryford. It's small, but perfectly formed, as they say. It's ideal for me and Binks and the best thing is that there's no commute. I just have to roll out of bed and I'm at work.'

Once again, an erotic image flickered across Millie's vision of Zach stretching his limbs as he made his way into the shower before he started his day ensuring the smooth running of his employers' Cotswold estate. Zach had already told her a little about his childhood, growing up in the Oxford-shire countryside with his younger brother, Martin, exploring the rivers and streams like a pair of water otters until the shock announcement that the family were relocating to the metropolis of London so his father could take up a management position in one of the large international law firms. His parents had divorced a couple of years later after his mother had discovered his father was having an affair with a colleague twenty years his junior.

Zach taste-tested the bolognese sauce for flavour, added an extra sprinkle of oregano and declared himself happy. He carefully replaced the jar in its rightful space in the cupboard, washed the spoon, dried it, and returned it to the cutlery drawer before removing the pan of cooked pasta and dumping its contents into a colander in the sink.

The whole scene was like a choreographed culinary ballet and Millie had to smother a smile as she watched him divided the spaghetti into a couple of wide-brimmed china bowls, add a dollop of sauce precisely into the centre of each, grate a generous helping of parmesan before adding a final garnish of fresh basil leaves. He then submerged the pan in the sink, repeated the performance he'd enacted with every other utensil, and joined Millie at the table with a second bottle of wine.

The aroma of garlic wafted to her nostrils and Millie clamped her lips together for fear of drooling. She had to admit that Zach Barker was turning out to be a man of surprisingly diverse skills, and as she twirled her spaghetti around her fork, she cast a surreptitious glance to the bookcase as heat flooded her cheeks once more.

Was one of the books *The Kama Sutra*?

Chapter Five

'Where do you think they've got to?' asked Ella, slinging her tea towel over her shoulder and glancing at the clock next to the powder-blue Smeg refrigerator. 'Everyone's usually here by nine-thirty for a ten o'clock start and it's almost eleven now.'

'Do you think they're perhaps disappointed with the Chocolate and Confetti course and are just too polite to say anything?' suggested Millie.

'No, of course not. Imogen told me that she's loving the tutorials. Maybe their hire car has broken down. You know what the roads are like round here, those cars do take a battering. Why don't you give Imogen a call?'

Millie grabbed her mobile and selected Imogen's number. Anxiety gnawed at her stomach as she waited for her to pick up. However, the phone went straight to voicemail and she decided not to leave a message. She inhaled a deep breath, but she felt like a slab of concrete was pressing all the oxygen from her lungs as she contemplated the possible reasons behind the women's failure to turn up for their third day at the Paradise Cookery School. Then another, even more alarming, thought occurred to her. What if one of them had food poisoning? That would definitely jeopardise any further classes.

'There's no point in fretting until we know what the problem is,' counselled Ella, gifting Millie with a wide smile. 'Let's grab some breakfast and sit outside on the veranda while we wait.'

Within minutes of sitting down under a parasol with her freshly ground coffee and flaky croissant, Millie's phone buzzed.

'Millie? Is that you?'

'Hi, Imogen. Is everything okay? Ella and I were worried about you.'

There was a pause at the other end of the line during which Millie heard what she thought was a gulp.

'I'm really sorry about this morning, Millie. But the most dreadful thing has happened.' Again, there was a brief silence whilst Imogen gathered her courage to continue. 'There was fire in the hotel kitchen in the early hours of the morning.'

'Oh my God! Was anyone hurt?'

'No. Thankfully the staff caught it before it had chance to spread from the dessert preparation area, but… but the thing is… my wedding cake has been totally destroyed – unless you like your cake with a chargrilled coating and flavoured with smoke. Not only that, but all the wedding favours Mum and Karen have painstakingly prepared were in a box next to the cake and every single one of them is ruined. It's a complete disaster. Mum's absolutely gutted but Brad is doing a grand job of comforting her – he's turning out to be a complete godsend, to be honest. Even Karen has come around to the view that he's great for Mum.'

'Oh, Imogen, I'm so sorry. What a nightmare. Is there anything Ella and I can do to help?'

'Thanks for the offer, but I don't think so. Jerome, the hotel manager, is very apologetic and has promised to come up with something for the cake-cutting ceremony. But, do you know what? He actually had the cheek to suggest a cardboard model and Photoshop! He changed tack pretty sharpish when he saw the look of fury on Mum's face. She asked why the hotel's chefs couldn't come up with something, but they're working flat out to clean the kitchen and feed the guests. It's a miracle none of the cooking equipment was affected so, after everything has been washed and sterilised, we can at least still have the wedding reception here on Sunday.'

'I'm really sorry, Imogen. Can't your wedding planner sort something out for you? Isn't this the kind of thing she should be used to troubleshooting? I bet she's got loads of ideas and contacts.'

'You'd think so, wouldn't you? But Mum, as usual, was right about Fleur Markham. She hasn't even turned up at the hotel yet. One of the waiters let slip that she's famous for her unreliability – now he tells us! I've tried to call her a few times but she's not answering her mobile. Mum thinks Jerome and Fleur have some personal history because she caught them arguing down by the gazebo last night when she was out with Brad for another of their romantic moonlit strolls. If that's true, you'd think they would keep their squabbles to themselves until the wedding is over. Mum's paying Fleur a hefty fee for her services, to make sure everything runs smoothly and every detail is perfect. So far, I don't think she's delivered anything we can't do ourselves! I think we can kiss goodbye to the kaleidoscope of butterflies Mum wanted – but to be honest, I'm not sure that's a bad thing.'

Imogen attempted a rueful laugh but instead burst in tears.

'Everything is going wrong. I knew Alex and I should have stood up to Mum and insisted on an intimate ceremony at home with a few close friends, instead of coming out here. I just wanted her to be happy, to be involved in the organising because I knew how much she would miss Dad. Perhaps Alex and I should cancel the whole thing. Maybe this is a sign…'

'Imogen… Imogen, please don't say that. It'll all work out fine,' Millie reassured her, her heart pounding out a symphony of sympathy for the distraught bride-to-be who should by rights be relaxing on a sun lounger with a pina colada instead of stressing over the wedding arrangements.

Millie flicked a quick glance to where Ella sat, sipping her Blue Mountain coffee, her brown eyes widening as she listened intently to the unfolding saga. She gave Millie a smile and a nod of approval.

'Look, I have an idea. When you feel up to it, why don't you come over to the villa with anyone who needs a bit of distraction and we'll spend the remaining three days of the Chocolate and Confetti course baking up a storm? Ella and I have made dozens of wedding cakes in our time. I can't promise you a brigade of sugar-paste butterflies or a froth of lavender-flavoured buttercream roses, but I'm sure we can produce something to wow your guests.'

'You and Ella are offering to bake me a wedding cake by Sunday?'

'Yes. And I've got a suggestion for the wedding favours too. How does three dozen wedding-themed cake pops sound? We can mould them into miniature bride-and-groom shapes. My friend Poppy showed me how to decorate them with coloured chocolate melts and they look amazing. We'll wrap them in cellophane, tie them with colour-co-ordinated ribbons, and your guests can take them home as souvenirs.'

'Wow! That sounds fabulous. Do you think it'll work?'

'I'm sure of it.'

'You are really kind to offer to do this, Millie. I'll have a chat to Alex and Mum and we'll be right over. A day filled with manic baking is exactly what I need to settle my nerves. Thank you, thank you, thank you – from the bottom of my heart.'

'It's a pleasure.' Millie sighed as she placed her phone in her lap and met Ella's gaze.

'I take it we've just been promoted from luxury cookery course presenters to deliverers of confectionary dreams?' Ella expelled a deep belly laugh that made Millie smile too. 'Well, we'd better get cracking on a shopping list. I'll give Denise a call and she can source whatever we need in Castries.

I'll ask Henri to drive up there and collect everything during his lunch hour. There's just one thing I'm confused about, though.'

'What's that?'

'What in sweet heaven's name is a cake pop?'

Millie laughed. 'It's a mini ball of chocolate cake on a stick – a bit like a lollipop – dipped in melted chocolate and decorated with, well, with anything you want really. You can mould them into a variety of shapes to create miniature birds, fish, hearts and flowers. I've made a batch for a Christmas party before that included snowmen with top hats and these fabulous mini Christmas puddings with sprigs of holly.'

'Okay. I think I'd better leave that side of things to you. Denise and I will get cracking on creating the best wedding cake this side of the Caribbean. I assume you realise that it's going to take every spare minute of our time to pull this off. You certainly know how to live a high-octane life, Amelia Harper!'

'Oh no, what catastrophe has Manic Millie visited upon us today?' asked Zach, who had caught Ella's last few words as he arrived on the veranda with Binks, who had a moth-eaten ball clenched in his jaw.

'Nothing to do with me this time.' Millie laughed.

'Where is everyone? I thought today was chocolate savouries day? Have you frightened your students away with all the culinary clutter?'

Zach grabbed a deckchair next to Ella and helped himself to one of the croissants. He tore it into two pieces, catching the crumbs on a plate, and popped one half in his mouth before tossing the other half to a very grateful Binks.

'As a matter of fact, Zachary Barker, Millie has just come to the rescue of our bride-to-be by offering our services to bake the most important cake in a woman's life!'

Zach rolled his eyes at Ella and would probably have scoffed if it had been Millie who had uttered such an outrageous statement. 'I know you're both totally obsessed with all things chocolate and sugar-related, but don't tell me that cake is in any way an *essential* part of anyone's life.'

'It is when it's your wedding cake!'

'What do you mean? Surely Imogen hasn't asked you to make her wedding cake four days before she's due to say "I do"?'

Millie explained as succinctly as possible what had happened at the hotel kitchen. As she was speaking, a sudden flame of doubt ignited in her

70

abdomen. Was Zach right to be sceptical? Could she really pull this off? Her heart had gone out to Imogen when she'd heard the obvious distress in her voice and she hadn't had time to think through her suggestion properly. Whilst she *had* made celebration cakes many times before, she hadn't made one since… well… since her own engagement. That cake had sat, in all its sugar-coated majesty, on a china pedestal in pride of place in the middle of the village hall where her party was being held – never to be cut. In fact, thinking back, she wasn't entirely sure what had happened to it. The most likely explanation was that her mother had spirited it away so as not to have it in the house as a constant reminder of her abandonment.

'She has, and Ella and I intend to deliver the most fabulous cake we can!'

'Oh no, Binks my friend. We'd better take cover! I dread to think what maelstrom of culinary mania is about to be visited on Claudia's pristine kitchen today,' Zach teased, a twinkle of mischief in his mahogany eyes and the cute dimples appearing to bracket his lips.

'Oh my God! Claudia! I'll have to call her to tell her what's happened. Do you think she'll object to what we're going to do, Ella?'

'Of course not, dear,' chuckled Ella. 'She'll be proud of us. It's exactly what she would have done herself. Ignore Zach.' Ella gave him a mock-stern glare. 'So what if there's a little bit of chaos if it means the work gets done? It's not as though we'll be pressing *his* kitchen in the lodge into action, is it?

'Heaven forbid!' exclaimed Zach, genuinely horrified at the thought.

Millie thought of the immaculately kept cabin that was Zach's temporary home whilst he cared for the cocoa plantation in his colleague's absence. Every time she set eyes on the place it became less like a land-based dwelling, more like a wooden steamer, moored on stilts against the backdrop of the lush splendour of the rainforest. Zach was probably one of the tidiest, most methodical people she had ever encountered – therefore her complete opposite. She smiled when she thought of her tendency to produce clutter and clumsiness and Zach's regular exasperated assertions that she could bring chaos to an empty room.

But their differences didn't stop there. Despite having grown to accept the leaden skies and rain-soaked streets of Oxfordshire and London, she still continued to crave the long, sunshine-filled days of Provence where her mother had been born and where she had spent a carefree childhood. Yet a close second in her hit parade of desirable locations had to be the Caribbean, and St Lucia in particular – an island of such beauty it whipped her breath away.

'Okay, well, I can't sit here chatting all day.'

Millie had to suppress a giggle when Zach pushed back his chair, picked up his plate and carried it into the kitchen where he rinsed it, dried it with one of Claudia's signature tea towels, and returned it to its allotted space in the cupboard next to the fridge. She also noticed that his meticulous tendencies extended to his attire, but despite his immaculately ironed lilac polo shirt and pristine black jeans screaming sartorial fastidiousness, they also served to enhance his attractiveness and once again she felt a flutter of desire in her lower abdomen.

Zach called Binks to heel then paused on the steps leading down to the pool.

'I know I'm probably going to regret saying this, but if you need any help with the washing up at the end of your bake-a-thon today, you can count me and Binks in – especially if there's going to be a selection of tasty titbits on offer for the workers.'

'Thanks, Zach, that's very kind of you,' said Ella before Millie had the chance to refuse – not that she had any intention of doing so. She knew they were going to need all the help they could get if they were going to have any chance of success.

'Right, I'll leave you to get *organised*,' smirked Zach. 'See you later. I'll bring my own rubber gloves.'

Millie watched him go, her eyes fixed on his muscular thighs and the way his jeans moulded his buttocks, not to mention the impressive bulge of his biceps from his daily workouts around the plantation. However, what was uppermost in her mind was how, despite his propensity to tease her at every opportunity, whenever he and Binks were around she felt lighter, more energetic, and *happy*. Against all her expectations, she realised that her feelings for Zach had morphed from friendship into something altogether more vibrant and she was enjoying every minute of her new-found lust for life and the people in it.

Chapter Six

'Hi? Millie? Is it okay to come in?' asked Imogen, her voice tight with repressed emotion.

'Of course, of course. Let me introduce you to Denise, Ella's best friend and fellow Caribbean cook extraordinaire. She's very kindly agreed to come over to the Paradise Cookery School for the day to help Ella make a start on your wedding cake.'

'Hello, Imogen, it's good to meet you,' beamed Denise from her position behind the demonstration bench, her hands thrust deep in a bowl of flour. Modelling her attire on the colours of the St Lucian flag, Ella's best friend had clearly been bestowed with a large slice of the body-confidence pie. Her hair was hidden by a gold, blue and black striped turban and, like Ella, she too favoured bold-is-beautiful necklaces. She exuded jollity, and despite having dropped everything to come to Ella's rescue, there was not a trace of stress on her smooth, wrinkle-free face.

'Hi, Denise. I can't tell you how grateful I am that you're all doing this for me.'

Millie's heart gave a flip of sympathy as she saw Imogen gulp down her emotions and offer them a grateful smile. Smudges of tiredness had appeared beneath her eyes, which were suspiciously pink from the tears she had inevitably shed since she had received the upsetting news about the hotel's kitchen fire.

'It's no problem at all, my dear,' said Ella, gathering Imogen into her arms, her multi-coloured bangles jangling around her wrist as she gave her a bear hug before resuming mixing the cake batter. 'I'm so sorry about what happened to your wedding cake, I hope the hotel is investigating the cause?'

'Jerome has promised to report back to Alex as soon as he can. Mum's acting like a whirling dervish: issuing orders, demanding answers, making lists, checking what still needs to be done before Sunday. She's even found the address of Fleur's office in Castries and has arranged for Brad to drive her over there so she can give her a piece of her mind. I wouldn't like to be anywhere in the vicinity when that conversation happens. Karen and Gracie are going to spend the day printing off some of the photographs Carla's taken of me and

Alex and turning them into bunting for decorating the gazebo, so I'm afraid there's only me, Carla and Harriet as your willing apprentices – just point us in the right direction and we'll get to work. I know that the best thing for me to do at the moment is to keep busy.'

'Okay. I think you should be on wedding cake duties so that Ella and Denise have an idea of the sort of design you'd like. Denise called in a favour and she's managed to get a whole carton filled with fresh flowers to decorate the table and cake stand. Ella's suggested a triple-tiered chocolate cake coated with fondant icing in white chocolate, milk chocolate and dark chocolate decorated with chocolate flowers and hearts.'

'Oh, that sounds perfect.' Tears glistened on Imogen's lower lashes as she snatched up an apron and set to work in between Ella and Denise sifting the flour and cocoa.

'So, what do you have planned for us, Millie?' asked Carla, strolling into the kitchen after snapping a few extra photographs of the Pitons from the villa's veranda. 'You know, I don't think I'll ever grow tired of looking at this view. It has everything a professional photographer could wish for: the azure of the ocean, the emerald of the forest, the elegant sweep of the bay, the terracotta roofs of the town nestled below the majesty of the Pitons. I can totally understand why Claudia has called this The Paradise Cookery School.'

'Come on, Carla. We're supposed to be helping Millie with the baking,' chastised Harriet, collecting her hair in her hands and tying it back with a band.

'Okay, so we'll be spending the day making cake pops. We need to whip up a few chocolate sponge cakes first. When they're cool, we'll crumble them, add frosting and mould them into shape on these sticks. Then we'll pop them in the freezer for an hour or so before we decorate them.'

'What on earth are cake pops?' asked Carla, slotting her hair behind her ears and pushing up the sleeves of her turquoise T-shirt.

'I think it might be best if I just showed you.'

Millie scrolled through her phone until she found an image of wedding-themed cake pops displayed in a painted flowerpot covered with confetti. Half of the cake pops had been decorated as a bride, the moulded chocolate cake dipped in white chocolate with a painted veil and finished off with a tiny pearl necklace. The other half represented the groom, complete with top hat and a cute pink bow tie.

'Oh my God – they are gorgeous! Why haven't I discovered cake pops before now! They look too good to eat. Ah, look, there's a cake pop poodle. It's adorable. Oh, and is that a goldfish with a crown? Oh, Carla, we've got to make some of those heart-shaped ones, too, and a few of…'

'Hold on,' interrupted Millie, laughing at Harriet's enthusiasm. 'We're making these for Imogen and Alex's wedding guests. We've got thirty-six to make, wrap in cellophane and tie with colour-co-ordinated ribbons. If we have any time at the end, we can experiment with other shapes.'

The three girls spent the next hour whipping up a dozen sponge cakes to form the interior of the cake pops before crumbling them into a large bowl and adding melted chocolate and chopped hazelnuts.

'Gracie would absolutely love to do this,' declared Carla.

'She'd probably make a better job of it, too. No offence, Carla, but your bride and groom combos look like a pair of boobs.'

'Do you think?' laughed Carla, squeezing the lumps of cake mixture on the end of her lollipop stick into pointed twin peaks.

'Okay, that's forty. We'll pop them into the freezer to harden and we'll decorate them later. So, what do you want to make with the mixture we have left?'

'I want to make Gracie one of those cute pink owls,' said Harriet, pointing to the photograph on Millie's phone.

'And I'm going to make Greg one of those sharks,' grinned Carla. 'Perfect!'

Imogen joined them and they indulged in a session of creativity and laughter, like a group of primary school children let loose on the craft table. They rolled the cake mixture into spheres the size of golf balls, stuck in a lollipop stick, and then sculpted them into a myriad of shapes.

'I used to love working with play dough when I was a child. It's so therapeutic. You know, all it takes is a couple of hours of baking and the stress and worry of this morning has melted away. So what if we haven't got a traditional fruit-filled wedding cake covered in marzipan and royal icing? It's not the end of the world. In fact, don't tell Mum I said this but I think I prefer the cake Ella and Denise have made.'

'What are the guys doing today?' asked Millie, tossing a tea towel on top of the pile of washing up waiting for attention on the end of their workstation.

'They're hiking up Gros Piton then spending the afternoon at the Sulphur Springs indulging in a mud bath. Alex did offer to go to Castries with Mum and Brad, but Mum didn't want him to miss the expedition. He's been looking forward to the hike since Greg booked it. They're expecting us to join them at The Blue Orchid in Soufrière for cocktails when we're finished here.'

'So, Imogen, how did you and Alex meet?'

'You'll love this, Millie,' said Carla, washing her hands and retrieving her camera to take a few snaps of the fish-shaped cake pop she had made for Greg that looked more like a melancholic manatee than a ferocious shark.

Imogen laughed, her eyes alight with happiness at being given the opportunity to talk about her fiancé. 'We met on the London Eye, would you believe?'

'Ask her to tell you the details,' said Harriet, popping a huge chunk of white chocolate in her mouth and rolling her eyes in ecstasy.

'Okay, ladies. I think we're finished baking for the day. Why don't you grab one of Denise's cocktails and take your gossip out onto the veranda to enjoy the view,' suggested Ella in her sing-song Caribbean accent, its cadence more pronounced after a long day spent on her feet. Despite Millie's cajoling, Ella had refused to shelve her addiction to heels and had steadfastly continued throughout the day in a pair of scarlet heels that clashed winningly with her voluminous orange and yellow kaftan.

Ella shooed the four women out of the kitchen to give her the chance to make adjustments to the six huge chocolate cakes that were cooling on wire racks on the demonstration workbench. She and Denise had decided to double-up the recipe so they could choose the best one of each size to decorate.

With a sigh of relief, Millie selected a Paradise Daiquiri made from local rum, freshly squeezed lime juice and sugar syrup, and sank into a deckchair overlooking the pool. It was five o'clock and she had been concentrating so hard on that day's bakes that she hadn't noticed the arrival of the daily deluge. The wooden boards on the veranda were dotted with puddles and the air held a distinct aroma of damp earth with a floral top note from the garland of roses that grew around the French doors. The parrots had resumed their cacophony of early evening chatter and Millie sent up a quick missive of gratitude to her personal director of fate that she was in such amazing place surrounded by a group of wonderful people.

'So, how come you met on the London Eye?'

Imogen took a sip of her pina colada and ran the tip of her tongue along her lower lip before launching into her story. 'Well, one of my customers loved the wedding jewellery she'd commissioned so much that she gave me tickets for a VIP experience in one of the pods. I have to confess, I'm not keen on heights, but I'm even less keen on enclosed spaces. I thanked her, of course, but I had no intention of going.'

'But I persuaded her,' said Carla, zooming in on a pot of pink and white geraniums on the steps leading to the swimming pool.

'It was fate,' added Harriet.

'When we arrived at the wheel to check in, we were informed that our pod had been double-booked...'

'Or Carla had got the time wrong...'

'It turned out that Alex's company had also reserved the pod to entertain a couple of clients but the clients hadn't showed, so they suggested we join them.'

'Immie was going to refuse, but I leapt at the chance,' said Carla, taking up the story. 'One of the guys was *hot, hot, hot*. I made a bet with Harriet that I could wangle a date with Mister Blue Eyes by the time the wheel had completed its rotation.'

'It was before Greg came on the scene,' Harriet explained to Millie.

'Yes. Harriet is to blame for introducing me to Greg,' said Carla, her eyes narrowed in fake irritation.

'Carla!'

'Anyway,' interrupted Imogen. 'We all piled into the pod. There were the three of us and Josie – one of my friends from Pilates – and Alex and four of his colleagues. It was a bit awkward at first and I was getting more and more uncomfortable as the pod travelled higher and higher. But we got chatting and it turned out Alex had studied architecture at uni so he took pity on me and started to point out all the landmarks on the London skyline – which was great until we reached the highest point and my knees just crumpled.'

Imogen's face took on a dreamy expression as she recalled what had clearly been, for her, the most momentous day of her life.

'Alex caught me and talked me through how safe we were. By the time I looked out of the window again we were on our way back down and I started to relax. He told me about the four years he'd spent in the army before joining his uncle's architects' practice in the City. You know how sometimes you feel as though you've known someone for years, when something just sort of clicks? Well, that's what happened with Alex. Carla thinks it's ridiculous but I knew straight away that I'd met my soulmate. When we got back to terra firma, Alex asked for my number. He called the next day to ask me to go to the women's quarter finals at Wimbledon with him. We've been together ever since.'

'And I met Owen through Alex,' said Harriet, sipping her mango mojito and staring out at the Pitons. 'He was still undergoing rehab after he'd been medically discharged from the army. I'm a sports physio so I was interested in what kind of therapy the army physios had planned to help him get back to peak fitness.'

'Did I hear you say Owen was a doctor?' asked Ella when she and Denise joined them on the veranda with a huge glass jug of freshly squeezed lemon-and-lime juice crammed with crushed ice and a handful of fragrant mint leaves.

'Yes, he was an army medic before he was injured when the vehicle he was travelling in was hit by a roadside bomb while he was stationed in Afghanistan. He almost lost his leg. Apparently, he now has more metal in his ankle than bone.'

'Ergh,' cringed Carla, turning her lips down-wards in a grimace as she rubbed her palms along her forearms to erase the goosepimples. 'I could never be a medic!'

'He was one of the lucky ones, though,' murmured Harriet, a shadow of sadness flitting across her expression. 'Ever since the accident Owen's hated driving any kind of vehicle. It's just the way the trauma of what happened affects him. He's got a great little scarlet-red MG, but he prefers to use public transport whenever he can. I usually do all the driving at home, but I'm terrified of driving abroad so Owen agreed to drive the hire car from the airport to the hotel. He hated it and he's made me promise that we'll get a taxi back when it's time to leave.'

'Don't worry, Harri, you can come with me and Greg in the Jeep. However, I feel it's my duty to warn you in advance – he drives like he lives – without fear or favour. I think he might have been Guy Martin's cousin in a former life.'

'How did you and Greg get together?' asked Millie, finishing her cocktail and refilling her glass with the home-made lemonade.

'Greg met Owen when he was stationed in Helmand Province. Harriet very kindly set us up on a blind date. I loved his zest for life, his willing-ness to try anything and give it his best shot. It's as though he's squeezing every last morsel out of the time he has to honour all those friends who didn't make it home. It's just that sometimes he can go a bit too far.'

'Who can blame him?' said Denise, her dark brown eyes filled with compassion.

'Alex and Owen know what he's like. It's just that when I introduce him to my friends and their partners he's so full-on he tends to terrify them,' Carla laughed, but her expression had softened.

'So, Millie.' Imogen swivelled round in her chair to face her, her pale blue eyes crinkling with interest. 'What's going on with you and Zach? And don't say nothing because I've seen the way he looks at you.'

'What do you mean?'

Heat seeped into Millie's cheeks and she shot an anxious look at Ella, who simply offered her a calm smile in return.

'You know exactly what I mean,' laughed Imogen, warming to her mission of interrogation. 'In fact, I thought you two were never going to climb out of that ditch you ended up in yesterday. You both looked very comfortable lying there with your arms wrapped around each other, his lips inches from yours. I definitely sensed a sparkle of electricity between the two of you. Are you…'

'Hey, hey, leave the girl alone, Immie!' giggled Harriet. 'Can't you see she's uncomfortable? Just because you're all loved-up with your handsome prince doesn't mean we all want to start feathering our love nests.'

'But she wants to...' teased Carla, eyeing Millie carefully before raising her camera lens and taking a quick snap.

Fortunately, Ella decided it was time to come to Millie's rescue before she melted from embarrassment. 'Girls, girls. It's six o'clock. I think the guys will be wondering where you've got to if you don't get a move on. Weren't they expecting you at The Blue Orchid at five-thirty?'

Imogen took the hint. 'Why don't you join us, Millie? You'd be very welcome. You too, Ella and Denise. The drinks are on Alex and I as a token of our appreciation for everything you've done for us today.'

'That very kind of you, dear, but look, that's my Henri.' Ella indicated the tiny red Fiat struggling to make its way up the steep driveway to the villa, a familiar calypso tune thrumming from the open windows. 'He's come to take me and Denise home. I'm sorry, Millie. I'm afraid we're going to have to leave you with the clearing up.'

'Oh, don't worry. It's definitely my turn.'

Millie waved off Ella and Denise with Henri and then watched the three girls tumble, laughing and giggling, into their hire car for their trip down to Soufrière and their rendezvous with the men.

She made her way from the courtyard back to the kitchen and surveyed the workbenches. A long sigh escaped her lips. It would take her until bedtime to wash everything up and return it to its allocated space ready for the next day. After consuming two of Denise's potent rum cocktails, her head felt like it had been stuffed with cotton wool so she decided her first job should be to make a cafetière of her favourite Blue Mountain coffee.

After a couple of gulps, she felt her energy seep back into her veins. She filled a bowl with soapy water and knelt down on the floor, her buttocks high in the air, rocking from side-to-side to the reggae rhythms blasting from the radio as she washed the marble floor tiles until they shone.

'Great view! Do you welcome all the Paradise Cookery School's guests like this? I'm not sure it's the best marketing strategy if you want repeat bookings. What do you think, Binks?'

'Woof!'

Chapter Seven

Millie scrambled upright too quickly and had to grasp onto the countertop to stop herself from falling. She had been working non-stop in the humid kitchen for eight hours with only a short break for a couple of cocktails. Her stomach rumbled in objection to the lack of consideration for lunch and she rubbed her palm over her eyes to erase the stars that were floating across her vision.

'Hey, are you okay? Here, why don't you sit down for a minute.'

'I'm fine. It's just been a really long day.'

'Looks like you've been experimenting with culinary pyrotechnics! How can so few people make so much mess? When I offered to help you tidy up earlier I didn't think the place would be taken over by a bunch of baboons enjoying their annual picnic.'

Millie tried to assess the disarray through Zach's eyes. The demonstration bench where Ella, Denise and Imogen had spent the day preparing the replacement wedding cake was spotless. Every mixing bowl, spatula and whisk had been washed, dried and returned to its rightful place in the cupboard, and the marble worktop had been wiped down until it sparkled in the last rays of the setting sun. The chocolate cakes sat in descending order on a wire rack to cool beneath three huge glass domes to prevent them from becoming a passing bug's gourmet evening meal. She knew Ella and Denise had also whipped up the three varieties of buttercream, which would be piped into rosette swirls the next day before the final embellishments of chocolate hearts and butterflies were scattered on the sides.

However, when Millie swung her gaze to the benches on her left and right where she had instructed Harriet and Carla in the art of creating cake pops, it was a completely different story – more in the horror than the romance genre. Whilst the cake pops were safely stored in the huge Smeg freezer, there were cake tins, spare lollipop sticks, snail trails of chopped hazelnuts, splodges of cocoa powder, and discarded coffee cups and cocktail glasses cluttering every available inch.

'It's not that bad. I've seen worse.'

'Now why doesn't that surprise me?'

Millie flicked the end of a tea towel at Zach's smirking face and experienced a swift arrow of desire jettison into her lower abdomen when he grabbed her wrist to stop her. He really was extraordinarily handsome, with his tousled ebony hair and eyelashes the colour of liquorice which, being blonde, she would give her eye-teeth to possess. Her fingertips tingled at his touch as she took in the dark golden hairs rippling over his forearms.

For several delicious moments she held his eyes, enjoying the way her heart fluttered against her ribcage and electricity reverberated in the space between them along with the heady fragrance of his lemony aftershave. However, what really ignited her senses was the way Zach was looking at her and the most natural thing in the world was to take a step forward to meet his lips. Unfortunately, her sudden movement dislodged a pyramid of china plates and, as if in slow motion, she watched a glass measuring jug tumble onto a pan handle which then catapulted its contents into the air, landing with a splatter at Binks's feet.

'Woof!' declared the delighted spaniel, licking up the surprise gift of icing and crumbs.

Millie raised her mortified eyes to Zach and waited for the inevitable pronouncement on her lackadaisical approach to culinary orderliness. She saw the corners of his lips twitch then he crumpled into laughter. She paused for only a couple of seconds, then joined in, laughing with him until tears sparkled on her lashes and the tension that had been building all day evaporated.

'Oh my God. Mishap Millie strikes again! You are a complete liability. What on earth have you been baking in here this afternoon?'

'Ella made those chocolate cakes, and I made over fifty cake pops which are setting in the freezer.'

'Cake pops? No, don't bother. Let's just get started on the chores or we'll be here all night. You take the washing up and I'll dry and put away. Here.'

To Millie's amazement, Zach produced a pair of bright pink Marigolds from his back pocket. Now it was her turn to smirk.

'Are you seriously expecting me to believe that you wear Marigolds when you wash up your dinner plates?' An image of Zach standing at his sink in a frilly apron sporting a pair of rubber gloves floated across her mind and she had to quash a rising giggle. 'What's the matter? Worried about your manicure?'

Zach rolled his eyes in reply and started to rummage in the drawers for one of Claudia's signature yellow tea towels. Whilst he had his back to her, Millie took the opportunity to continue with her appreciation of his impressive physique. At six feet two inches, there wasn't a spare inch on his frame, yet she knew his muscular body had not been achieved from anything as boring as sweating over the equipment in a gym, but from working the land.

An unexpected image of Luke flitted across her mind. Her former boyfriend hadn't been blessed with the height gene so he had made up for his lack of stature with a forceful personality. He was slender too, but that was because he had no interest in consuming the food he lavished so much care and attention on creating. Why hadn't she seen that as odd?

Also, Luke was as fair as Zach was dark; any contact with the sun turned his skin an unattractive shade of ripe tomato on the rare occasions she had been able to persuade him to leave the restaurant they ran together for a trip to the beach or country-side when the sun was shining. The final item on Millie's list of contrasts was the fact that Luke had steadfastly refused to entertain the possibility of owning a pet. She would have loved a dog or a cat. In fact, even a hamster would have done but there had been no persuading him.

Whilst Millie loaded the dishwasher with the kitchen utensils, Zach filled the sink with hot soapy water to wash the glasses. To the smooth rhythm of the Caribbean music drifting from the radio, they worked in easy harmony until every last piece of cutlery and crockery had been returned to its resting place ready for use the following day. When Millie finally hung up her apron, she had to admit it was a very satisfying feeling to see the kitchen returned to its chaos-free glory. Fitz and his friends — the gang of builders Claudia had employed to upgrade the villa's kitchen — might have possessed a laid-back attitude to timekeeping, but their work-manship was exemplary.

Millie found a small aluminium bowl in the cupboard underneath the sink, filled it to the brim with fresh water, and offered it to Binks, who guzzled it noisily. She fondled his silky ears with affection as she watched Zach scrutinise the room like a surgeon in an operating theatre. She thought he was about to declare himself satisfied when he sighed, snatched up a slice of kitchen towel, and wiped away a miniscule splodge of ground coffee from the marble bench top.

'I think it's even tidier than when we started this morning!' she smiled. 'Thanks, Zach. Without your help I would have been here until well past midnight.'

'You're welcome. I did offer to help and I'm a man of my word. Anyway, I have an ulterior motive.'

'What sort of ulterior motive?'

Millie's stomach performed a backflip of anticipation and a whoosh of desire rotated through her body causing her skin to prickle. Her thoughts spun to her bedroom in the studio across the courtyard with cool white cotton sheets and muslin drapes floating at the window. But then her mind diverged onto a different tangent – knowing Zach, his intentions could equally involve the quad bikes lurking in the shed behind his lodge or the archery targets she had seen affixed to the coconut trees while on her early morning walks.

'Since you arrived on St Lucia, you've hardly taken any time off to explore the island. You're leaving on Monday and who knows when you'll get the chance to come back.'

'Well, I have been a little preoccupied with supervising the kitchen renovations and then presenting a luxury cookery course. Anyway, you did take me on that amazing trip to the Diamond Waterfalls last week…'

Millie felt her cheeks colour when she recalled their dash through the afternoon downpour to a remote shack in the rainforest that she was sure was used as a love nest by the locals. As they had waited for the rain to abate, Zach had confided a little of his personal history and offered her the opportunity to reciprocate. It had been too early in their friendship for her to reveal the details of her broken engagement, but Zach had not been as reticent about sharing the fact that his former girlfriend, Chloe, had become engaged to someone else within weeks of them splitting up. Their conversation in the tiny wooden shack under the rainforest canopy had been a turning point for her.

'The Diamond Falls are just one of many spectacular sights St Lucia has to offer. Are you up for another expedition?'

'Zach, I'd love to explore more of the island, but I just don't have the time if I'm going to get everything done before Imogen and Alex's wedding on Sunday...'

'What time is Imogen coming over tomorrow?'

'Around twelve o'clock, but...'

'Perfect. I've spoken to my friend François and he's expecting us at seven a.m. – that means a six o'clock start for us.'

'What exactly do you have in mind?'

'It's a surprise. Trust me. You'll love it. Come on, Binks, let's leave Millie to get a good night's sleep. By the way, I recommend you wear a long sleeve T-shirt and a pair of comfortable shoes – none of those sparkly flip-flops you're so fond of. Tomorrow, instead of affixing the badge declaring to the world that you are the Countess of Chaos and Cupcakes, or the Baroness of Buttercream and Brioche, you'll be given the opportunity to perform in the starring role of Millie, the Mistress of Misadventure!'

'Adventure? Zach I really don't…'

But he and Binks had already reached the end of the veranda and were ignoring her protestations. It was after seven o'clock and twilight decorated their duet of silhouettes with a golden glow until they disappeared into the trees.

Millie heaved a sigh, indecision flooding her brain. Okay, the kitchen was pristine and ready for another busy day at the coalface of the culinary world. The cake pops were ready to be decorated, and Ella and Denise had the wedding cake under control. But could she afford to abandon her post, even if it was only for a couple of hours before their guests arrived? She really wanted to show Claudia that she was not just capable of supervising the building work and delivering a finished product on time, but that she could also take charge of an upmarket cookery school and showcase the fabulous Caribbean recipes that her boss had specifically devised for the Chocolate & Confetti course.

Then something Ella had said earlier came screaming back to her. She should take some time to relax and have fun. Millie knew that her new-found contentment reflected in her disposition when she stood in front of the cookery school enthusiasts and encouraged even the most reluctant of students to grab their confidence and give the recipe a go. It had taken a mere few days in the St Lucian sunshine for her to discard the mantle of melancholy she had arrived with and replace it with a cheerful smile and a carefree demeanour. Being happy and being professional were not mutually exclusive; in fact she would even go as far as to say that they were a perfect partnership. As long as she made sure Zach knew she had to be back at the villa by eleven-thirty to be ready behind her demonstration bench at midday, then tomorrow couldn't come soon enough.

Chapter Eight

Millie tossed back the covers and crawled out of bed. She had just ten minutes to make herself presentable before Zach arrived. The sun was already peeking over the horizon, ready to make its debut in another sun-filled day. The dawn chorus had started on its second verse and she flicked the switch on the radio to add a soft calypso soundtrack to her morning shower.

As she dragged a brush through her voluminous curls, she decided that she would take a leaf out of Imogen's book and put her hair into a ponytail with the hair tie Poppy had given to her before she left London for the Caribbean. It felt like a lifetime ago since she'd sat with her best friend and gossiped about the patisserie and the next guy on Poppy's radar. She missed her and experienced a sudden urge to pick up her mobile and give her a call until she heard an impatient toot from the courtyard beneath the window of her tiny studio flat. Never mind, she thought, she would be seeing her in five days' time.

She grabbed a bottle of water from the fridge, slung her straw bag over her shoulder, and cantered down the stairs to meet Zach for her magical mystery tour of St Lucian highlights.

'Jump in!' Zach called through the open window of Tim's scarlet BMW roadster. 'Great to see you've heeded my advice about the sensible footwear.'

'No Binks today?'

'Can't take him where we're headed.'

Millie groaned. That didn't bode well. Perhaps Zach had hired a boat and they were going fishing, or worse, maybe he had organised a session of parasailing. A coil of trepidation began to weave through her abdomen but she shoved her fear to one side. It was pointless speculating what she was about to experience, so instead she decided to turn her attention to what was fast becoming one of her favourite pastimes – covertly appraising her companion as he expertly handled the twist and turns of the St Lucian roads through colourful villages and row upon row of banana and cocoa trees.

In profile, Zach was as attractive as ever in his navy shorts and immaculate boat shoes. The collar of his peppermint green polo shirt was open at the neck to reveal a smattering of chest hair. It occurred to her that whenever she was in the company of Zach Barker her emotions always churned uncontrollably, whether that was an overflow of annoyance and indignation whenever he accused her of causing chaos, unexpected surprise and delight when he offered to help her with the washing up, or a concoction of apprehension and sexual attraction that was whipping through her veins at the present moment.

Her inspection lingered on the way his long fingers draped across the steering wheel of the little sports car: sure, relaxed, confident. She recalled something that Carla had said about Greg – that he made her feel alive, and it was the same for her when she was with Zach. There was never a dull moment; either they were engaged in a battle of verbal sparring or he was challenging her to abandon her comfort zone and indulge in a brand new experience. She had a feeling that whatever he had organised for them that morning would involve plenty of physical exertion and mental agility – just like everything she did with Zach Barker.

Why had he insisted on keeping the activity they were about to experience a secret? But she knew the answer – he had expected her to refuse, to plead a more urgent engagement. And he was right. After all, she was a confirmed beach and sunshine addict whose idea of a good time was swinging in a hammock beneath a swaying palm tree with a cocktail in one hand and a good book in the other, *not* an intrepid tropical rainforest explorer!

Panic resumed its insidious journey around her body. She started to feel lightheaded and almost had a coronary when a hand-painted signpost for a local airfield loomed in front of them. Oh God! They were going skydiving! Her breath began to feel laboured and her heartbeat increased. She was about to die!

'Zach, I really don't think...'

'What's the matter? Your face is the colour of one of Ella's meringues! Are you okay?'

'I'm fine, it's just that I think *your* idea of having fun and *my* idea of having fun reside at opposite sides of the entertainment spectrum. Can't we just...'

'Are you telling me that the gutsy, *half-French* Amelia Harper is frightened to try something new? You're always telling me that you love experimenting.'

'In the kitchen, with flavours and textures and the most exotic, even outlandish, ingredients I can get my hands on? Yes! But I would never in my wildest nightmares contemplate for even one second hurling myself out of a plane in the name of experimentation.'

'A plane?' Zach shot a mischievous glance at the signpost that flashed by. 'You want to do a parachute jump?'

'No, I do not want to do a parachute jump!'

It was happening again. Her temper had been ignited and she opened her mouth to continue with a litany of justifications as to why she had no intention of throwing herself to her death. Her life might not be perfect after what had happened with Luke, but it was definitely on an upward trajectory at last. She loved her home in London. She adored her job at Étienne's little patisserie and had fun on her nights out on the town with Poppy. And she was absolutely loving presenting the cookery courses at the Paradise Cookery School for Claudia, not to mention being blessed with the friendship of Ella, Lottie and Denise.

Zach chuckled. 'Ah, there she is! Cantankerous Millie pokes her head above the parapet again. I love her!'

Millie gawped at him but before she could properly compute what he had just said to her, he had swung the car sharply to the left down a bumpy dirt track. She had to grab on to her seat to steady herself and the moment was lost. They had arrived at Treetop Adventures and the next, much more welcome sensation in her kaleidoscope of emotions, was relief. Although it wouldn't have been her first choice of activity for an early Thursday morning jaunt, it beat the spots off anything airborne.

'Are you ready to channel your inner eagle?'

'Do I have any choice?' she said as she slipped out of the passenger seat to greet Zach's friend François, who was waiting for them in the deserted car park. Dressed in khaki combat trousers and Doc Marten boots, he could easily have been cast in the role of International Man of Action – Caribbean-style.

'Hey, Zach, good to see you, man.' François offered Zach a fist bump, a broad grin splitting his cheeks as he led them to the little wooden cabin that housed his company's reception. 'And you must be Millie. Welcome to Treetop Adventures. I'm pleased to see Zach has managed to persuade you to give it a go. I can promise that you're in for an awesome ride!'

'Hi, François. Thank you, I'm really looking forward to it,' she improvised, hoping her expression didn't give away the fact that she was terrified. Heights had never been one of her strongest points.

'Had to keep Millie in the dark about our final destination, but I think as long as the activity doesn't involve throwing ourselves out of the back of an aeroplane we should be good to go.'

'Trust me, you'll love the zip-line! Here, put this helmet on and take these gloves with you.'

Millie smiled and took the safety equipment from François. She should have known Zach's 'exploring the island expedition' would be something like this. She cast her eyes around the rainforest clearing that housed the Treetop Adventures offices and shuddered when she saw the mountaineering gear through the open door of the on-site storeroom – a separate wooden structure at the back of the reception lodge. However, now that she was there she was determined to make the most of the ride that had been built on the St Lucian hillside.

It was only seven a.m. but already the humidity was rising. All around her, the lush tropical trees and plants crammed every spare inch of ground below what looked like a sky-high obstacle course. Shafts of diaphanous sunlight sliced through the branches overhead causing intricate shadows to dance on the forest floor. The aroma of coconut oil from her shampoo, and damp mulched bark, tickled her nostrils and the only sound, apart from the early morning echo of birdsong, was the persistent beat of her heart thumping through her eardrums.

At that time of the morning they had the place to themselves for which Millie was grateful. She really didn't want an audience for her approaching arboreal ordeal. Under François's careful instruction, they climbed into the harnesses, pulled on their helmets and stood in a clearing beneath the canopy of leaves for a short safety briefing, which Millie knew was solely for her benefit. She listened to every word, wishing she had a notepad and pen to jot down a few of his tips. But this was not an activity where you could take a quick peek at your notes if you got stuck and a helix of alarm began to wind its way up into her chest. She shoved it aside and raised her chin in the air. She was going to do this.

She plastered a smile on her lips and followed Zach and François to the wooden platform for her very first leap into the unknown. However, when she looked down and saw the zip wire dip steeply before disappearing into the dense congregation of trees, her stomach dropped like a penny down a wishing well.

'Okay, Zach, it's all yours. You know what to do. Have fun, Millie!'

She watched Zach leap from the platform and zoom down the wire with astonishing speed, the hum from the friction causing her nerves to sparkle. She tossed a glance over her shoulder at François, who gave her a brief nod of encouragement.

'Relax,' he smiled, clipping the carabiner onto Millie's pelvic harness. 'Just jump before you have time to think about it too much. Trust me – you'll love it!'

Millie wasn't so sure.

'Jump!'

And before she could formulate a cogent argument in support of a retreat to the lodge where she had seen cans of ice-cold lemonade, François had urged her forward. He must have detected her reluctance to tip her toes from the edge of the platform without persuasion, so he gave her a gentle push.

Seconds later, she was swept from the wooden tree-top balcony, the on-coming breeze whipping her fringe from her eyes and cooling the perspiration that had collected at her temples and beneath her breasts. She leaned back as François had instructed and the momentum of her weight took her whizzing through an emerald tunnel of dense forest. Her initial nervousness was swiftly overtaken by a feeling of exhilaration as she sailed through the leafy wilderness. By the time she landed in an undignified heap on the next platform, every trace of anxiety had vanished to be replaced by a feeling of accomplishment.

'Enjoy that?' asked Zach, offering her his palm to pull her upright.

'It was amazing!'

Their eyes met for a brief moment and Millie struggled with the intensity of the feelings that swirled through her body. The impulse to grab Zach and kiss him was almost too much to resist.

'Great. On to the second challenge then.'

Millie's eyes widened when she followed the direction of Zach's finger as he indicated the next part of their elevated obstacle course. Her knees weakened at the sight of the taut steel cables that sagged precariously through the vegetation to her right. She could just about make out the next platform through the hovering morning haze.

'Want me to go first again?'

'Please.'

She watched him fly through the air as though he was out on a Sunday stroll. When he arrived on the next wooden ledge he spun round and waved at her in encouragement.

'Your turn!'

This time there was no François standing next to her to encourage her to jump. She had to do this on her own. She gritted her teeth, relegated her swirling nerves to the crevices of her mind, and launched herself forward. Immediately the cables began to undulate and sway to the left and right. She clutched at the wires above her head like François had demonstrated in their safety briefing to slow her speed, allowing the errant branches to brush against her shins instead of whipping at her knees with sadistic zeal.

Wow – what a spectacular view!

Trees as tall as telegraph poles crowded the area, their trunks laced together with a cat's cradle of steel cables and ropes. The sun glanced from the glossy leaves of the banana plants, heavy with ripening fruit, and the local bird population launched from their homes squawking their objection to her invasion of their privacy. It was a perfect Caribbean paradise.

She was so busy drinking in the bucolic panorama that she had forgotten to prepare for her arrival. Within seconds, she had crashed into Zach as he waited to guide her onto the platform.

'Elegant!'

'Sorry,' she smiled, enjoying the feeling of his arms around her waist as he steadied her.

Sadly, her pride in her achievement was short-lived. When she chanced a peek over the edge to the ground below she experienced a sharp nip of vertigo, which sent her shooting backwards to glue her spine to the tree trunk, her stomach contracting around something akin to a miniature porcupine. Despite wearing gloves, her palms were already smarting from the friction caused by clutching onto the wire, but that was nothing compared to the twist of terror she felt when she saw how far up they were.

'It's probably best if you don't look down!' laughed Zach.

The fragrance of damp leaves and Zach's citrus-scented cologne pushed her senses into overdrive and she was suddenly overtaken by a bout of uncontrollable trembling. Zach grabbed her and pulled her into his chest, rubbing her back until her jitters passed. Her eyes locked onto his then dropped down to the curve of his lips. Whilst François's safety briefing hadn't specifically banned kissing, a shaky wooden platform ten metres from the ground wasn't the most appropriate place to indulge in a passionate embrace.

Thankfully the moment was broken by a shriek from an escaping parrot and before she knew what was happening, Zach was reattaching her clip to the next zip wire.

'Just remember to look straight ahead and enjoy the experience!'

She found Zach's eyes, taking strength from his silent support. She inhaled a steadying breath, then tipped her weight from the platform. Sweat trickled down her spine and her fringe stuck to her forehead beneath her helmet. However, she could feel the intensity of Zach's reassurance vibrate through the air, so she gathered every last ounce of courage she possessed and forced herself to enjoy the ride.

'Having fun?' Zach asked when he landed gracefully next to her.

'Erm…' she murmured.

'Don't worry, the best is yet to come. After you.'

Millie swallowed down the rampaging emotions the last few minutes had stirred and wriggled her toes to the edge of the final wooden platform – this time without being coaxed. Every one of her senses had been woken from their slumber. Every nerve ending tingled, every pore in her body exuded an unexpected surge of confidence. This time she leapt into the air with a whoop of excitement, feeling almost intoxicated by the exhilaration of soaring through the lush tropical canopy like a bird spreading its wings for the first time.

Her passage sent tree lizards and manicou scuttling from her path, and her hair flew high into the air from beneath the confines of her safety helmet. She even swung her legs to encourage extra speed until once again she landed in an unseemly heap on a mound of shredded bark that marked the end of their adventure.

'That was awesome!' she screamed as Zach landed next to her, his face alight with pleasure.

'Didn't I tell you that you'd have fun? And it's great to see the real Millie poking through that comfort blanket you're so determined to wrap yourself up in. You have to be prepared to squeeze the most out of every day, push your boundaries and grasp the world by the scruff of its neck. Otherwise we become stuck in a rut and who wants to live that kind of existence?'

Millie couldn't help herself. She was so overwhelmed by what she had achieved that morning that she slung her arms around Zach's neck and gave him a kiss — despite her determination to play it cool. She knew what he had said was right. She had been hiding beneath a cloak of misery after Luke had left her, and it was time to make some changes and move on.

'Thank you, Zach. That was the most amazing thing I've ever done. At this precise moment, I feel like I could do just about anything! Overcome any challenge that life throws in my direction. It was exactly what I needed.'

'You're welcome. However, this morning's excursion into new experiences is not over yet! Come on, I'll race you back to the car!'

Chapter Nine

As they wound their way down the hill back to civilisation, Millie slipped into a daydream. Whilst Zach's hands were clenched firmly on the steering wheel as he negotiated the sharp bends and avoided the huge potholes, she was still agonisingly aware of his proximity. Her throat was dry and her fingertips buzzed with anticipation whenever he glanced across and smiled. The way he looked at her made her feel special, that she was important to him and that he didn't want to be anywhere else other than by her side.

She had never expected to feel such a strong physical attraction to anyone so quickly after splitting with Luke and she struggled to understand how to react. The more time she spent with Zach, the harder it was to deny that she had developed a closeness with him that her relationship with Luke had lacked.

Nevertheless, the fact remained that her stay in St Lucia was temporary and despite her internal struggle to resist grabbing him and indulging in a kissing marathon right there and then, the last thing she wanted was to embark on a holiday romance because that way the progress she had made since arriving on the island, in all areas of her life – professional and personal – would be wound back to the beginning and she couldn't risk that.

Or could she? If she was aware from the outset that it was only going to be a fling, something short and deliciously sweet, then what harm would that do? In fact, it might just help her to paper over all the remaining cracks in her self-esteem that Luke's cheating had caused and producing a stronger, more resilient outlook over the romantic landscape.

She wondered what was going on in Zach's mind. There was no way he couldn't have noticed the chemistry between them; she had seen the scorching looks he gave her when he thought she wasn't looking. But what did that mean? He too had recently emerged from a relationship, although he and Chloe hadn't lived together and the reason they had separated was because she had demanded a commitment Zach hadn't been able to offer.

They reached the outskirts of Castries, the island's capital, and she knew immediately where Zach was headed. A smile tugged at the corners of her lips. Of course, he probably didn't know that she had been there before, but in any event, it was one of her favourite places on St Lucia so an unexpected repeat visit was going to be a real treat.

Even at that early hour the place bustled with a menagerie of people, some laden with bulging shopping bags, others pulling overburdened trollies, and others still lugging huge plastic crates piled with fish to their vehicles to feed hungry lunchtime tourists.

'Brace yourself for an assault on the senses!' declared Zach, swerving the car into the tiniest of parking spaces and leaping from his seat.

Millie didn't want to spoil Zach's fun so she kept quiet about her familiarity with Castries's famous outdoor market. Her spirits soared as she walked up the steps to be confronted by a kaleidoscope of colours. She paused on the threshold and took a moment to inhale the sweet smell of paradise floating on the air from the stall to her right: nutmeg, cinnamon, vanilla, star anise, ginger, a spice-filled medley of happiness in one sniff. She knew she would never be able to bake a batch of mince pies without thinking of this glorious market within whose walls were some of the freshest herbs and spices she had ever encountered.

They meandered down the rows of stalls, stopping so Millie could snatch up a woven jute bag embroidered with a map of the island from a smiling vendor who assured her that she had hand-sewn and decorated it herself. Armed with her basket, Millie succumbed to the insistent call of her shopping gene. She would have loved to be accompanied by her mother and sister with whom she liked to spend time mooching around the markets in Provence, but Zach turned out to be a fabulous substitute. He was knowledgeable and enthusiastic for the locally grown produce, and a great help with the inevitable bartering, not to mention carrying the three bottles of local rum she'd bought, one of which even had Poppy's name scrawled on the label!

'Planning a party or are these for personal use only? I feel obliged to warn you that that stuff's lethal in large doses.'

Millie laughed, feeling as though she was on a first date when everything around her seemed so much more intoxicating: the colours so vibrant, the aromas so evocative, the music swirling through the alleyways causing her hips to sway to the St Lucian rhythm.

'Christmas gifts for my sister and my friend, Poppy. I know Jen will probably use hers in one of her recipes, but Poppy will create the most delicious rum cocktails and it'll be finished before Boxing Day!'

'It's a great choice. I know my brother would prefer a bottle of Caribbean hooch rather than the sweater Mum knitted for him last year with a huge red reindeer's nose stuck on the front. You should have seen Martin and I on Christmas morning looking like a festive Tweedledee and Tweedledum — but if our sartorial road crash made her happy while she roasted the turkey, then it was no real hardship.'

Zach smiled but Millie noticed a shadow stalk across his eyes. She wondered what had caused it: the mention of his mother or his brother? She knew family dynamics could be battlegrounds but as they were having such a wonderful time she wasn't sure whether she should ask Zach to enlarge on anything so personal.

They had paused next to a stall selling home-made jewellery fashioned from polished pebbles and leather thongs. Millie thought immediately of Lottie, no doubt at that very moment rushing around the veranda of the Purple Parrot serving fragrant omelettes and rich dark coffee to its discerning patrons, and selected a necklace made from linked sea shells to give her as a goodbye present. When she handed over her money, her heart gave an uncomfortable lurch as she remembered she only had four days left on the island after which she would probably not see Lottie, Dylan or even Ella again.

'Fancy a coffee before we head off home?'

Millie checked her watch. 'I'd love one as long as we're not too long – I really need to get back to the villa before Imogen and her party arrive. That's if Imogen *does* decide to come today. They've got so much going on, I wouldn't be surprised if they cancelled so they can concentrate on the wedding arrangements. I wonder why the wedding planner's suddenly gone missing?'

'No idea. Come on, I need an injection of caffeine before tackling the drive to Soufrière.'

Zach indicated the patio outside a ramshackle café where a plump, jolly-faced woman, her dark hair streaked with silver, was busy brandishing a threadbare broom in a futile attempt to shoo away the dust and market debris from the pavement. As they approached, she ceased her melodious humming to offer them a wide welcoming grin, displaying a set of incongruously white teeth.

The sun was now well above the horizon, playing a game of hide-and-seek with a few gauzy clouds, and the temperature was climbing steadily.

They sat down at one of the tables and sipped the thick dark coffee the owner insisted they sample. Unsurprisingly, it was delicious and injected a welcome shot of energy into Millie's veins.

She felt so relaxed in Zach's presence. Even if she ignored the electric current that was zapping through the air between them, sitting there with her face turned towards the sun, she felt as though she had known him for years and not less than three weeks. In that short space of time, she had been able to share with him the most excruciatingly embarrassing episode of her life – the night Luke had ditched her at their engagement party for her best friend's mother. Until then, shame and mortification about what had happened had clung to her like a rash, so much so that whenever someone had looked at her for any length of time, she thought they could see it.

Of course, Poppy had had a hand in helping her to start coming to terms with the uninvited changes that had befallen her life, but she had been steadfast in her refusal to contemplate dating again. How could she trust someone with her heart after what had happened? But, strangely, unburdening her demons to Zach had ushered her much further down the path of acceptance, and the burning humiliation that had been persistently present before she'd hopped on the aeroplane had melted to an almost inconsequential item of ancient history.

Was it Zach or was it the island paradise she had been so fortunate to spend time in?

Whichever it was, Zach's presence had been an integral part of her emotional recovery and everything that had happened between them that morning at the zip wire ride was suddenly magnified sending her attraction to him into overdrive. There was no denying their relationship had moved on to a new level, and that because they had both had the courage to bare their souls on subjects they had previously hugged close to their chests, their honesty had drawn them together and eradicated any awkwardness. She met his eyes, her pulse racing, ready to express how she felt and to ask him how he felt about her, but before she even opened her mouth, Zach had checked his watch and jumped up from his chair.

'Come on, Marvellous Millie, we need to cart all this paraphernalia you've acquired back to the car. How many students did you say were on the Chocolate and Confetti course? I think you've bought enough to feed the whole of Soufrière!'

Millie smiled, bending down to collect the carrier bags filled with a mixture of treasures. She only hoped it would all fit in her suitcase! As Zach paid the bill, she resolved to have the conversation she planned on their journey back to the villa.

'So, what's on the itinerary of the Paradise Cookery School today? Macaroons? Petit fours? French horns?'

'French horns?' she giggled. 'You can't eat…'

'Just joking! Oh, hang on, hang on… I'd better take this.'

Zach grabbed his phone from the back pocket of his shorts and glanced at the screen. In the split second before he turned his back to take the call, Millie saw the shock written boldly across his handsome features.

'Hi. Chloe? Why are you…'

There was a pause.

'Here? You mean in St Lucia?'

Another pause.

'But…'

Millie was frozen to the spot. Surely the person on the other end of the phone couldn't be Zach's ex-girlfriend Chloe? The same Chloe who had terminated their relationship because Zach hadn't produced an engagement ring when she had suggested they moved on to the next level. Hadn't Zach told her that she had met someone else almost straight away who had proposed to her at the top of the Eiffel Tower? What was going on?

'Well, I don't see why you can't grab a taxi…'

Zach had now turned around to face Millie, his eyes holding her gaze with a mixture of alarm and dismay. She noticed that his cheeks had coloured and he was rubbing his palm across the stubble on his chin in consternation.

'Okay, okay. I'll be there in an hour.'

Zach cut the call and opened his mouth to speak but no words of explanation came forth.

'Was that Chloe, as in Chloe your ex-girlfriend?'

'Yes.'

'And?'

'She's just landed at the airport and wants me to collect her.'

'But I thought…'

However, Zach wasn't listening. He spun on his heels and started to make his way down the street to towards where they'd left Tim's car, leaving Millie to scramble in his wake with her myriad shopping bags.

The bubble of their early morning adventure had burst and the drive back to the villa was the most excruciating Millie had ever experienced. Awkwardness shimmered in the air between them and she only just managed to hang onto her urge to blurt out a litany of questions she wasn't even sure she wanted to hear the answers to. In the silence, her thoughts once again began to meander through the labyrinths of self-doubt that had been hewn by Luke's infidelity and she chastised herself for thinking things had changed.

Chapter Ten

'Hi, Millie! Oh, my God. What happened to your hair?' laughed Carla, taking in Millie's halo of honey-blonde curls that had ballooned to double its normal volume.

'The question you should be asking, Carla,' chuckled Imogen, kicking off her stilettos so she could pad into the villa's kitchen in her bare feet, 'is, *who* did that to Millie's hair. Millie, I saw you emerge from a very cute red roadster a few minutes before we arrived in the courtyard.'

Millie met Ella's gaze with what she hoped was a silent plea for protection from the interrogation Imogen was poised to pursue. Every nerve in her body sparkled with panic at the thought of either confessing what had happened that morning or having to conjure up something mundane enough not to attract further questioning. She went with the latter.

'Oh, I had to buy a few things at the market this morning so I got a lift back up the hill from a friend.'

Millie saw the scepticism in Imogen's eyes, clear evidence that she wasn't buying her explanation, but her expression swiftly changed to one of acceptance when she saw the faint shake of Ella's head. Unfortunately, Harriet didn't occupy the same empathy spectrum.

'I know, I know!' she squealed. 'She's been on a date with that hunky estate manager, Zach Barker. Yes, bingo! That's definitely a blush of guilt!'

'Oh, come on. Spill the details, Millie. I've been starved of gossip since I got here,' moaned Carla, smoothing her palm over her head and tucking the sides of her hair round her ears in that familiar gesture. Despite the fact that she was supposed to be there to bake, and decorate the wedding cake pops, her beloved Pentax was strung round her neck like an over-sized necklace. 'Unless you count what happened when Julia eventually managed to track down Fleur Markham's offices yesterday.'

'Why? What happened?' asked Ella, her ears pricking up at the mention of Imogen and Alex's elusive wedding planner, but she was equally keen to grasp onto a subject that would divert attention from Millie.

'Well, Mum's even more upset about her disappearance than I am. As you know, she and Brad took a taxi over to Castries yesterday to look for her offices, but when they got there the doors were locked and there was no sign of life. The girl in the flower shop downstairs, Martha I think her name was, said she hadn't seen Fleur since Sunday – that's the day we had our first meeting with her at the hotel, too.'

'What did you think of Fleur when you met her? Did you think she would be reliable?'

'That's the weird thing. Alex and I really liked her. She seemed to have everything under control. She showed us photographs of our bouquets and the flower arrangements she'd ordered for the tables, and she assured us that there was no problem with arranging the release of butterflies Mum wanted so much. Fleur said she'd been asked for a lot worse! She had the string quartet organised for the ceremony and the live band booked for the evening disco. Everything else is being sorted out by the hotel. So after she had met with us she had an appointment to talk through the arrangements with the hotel's temporary manager, Jerome. She seemed efficient and organised and very professional. We were due to see her on Wednesday to finalise the rehearsal on Saturday.'

'Yes, but remember what Julia said,' interrupted Carla, her green eyes wide with excitement. 'Didn't she hear Fleur arguing with Jerome in the gazebo?'

'Did she hear what they were arguing about?' asked Ella, her dark eyebrows raised with interest.

'I don't think so. And if it was anything to do with the wedding arrangements, I know Mum would have lurked in the bushes to listen in. She just sensed that the two of them had some personal history.'

'Maybe he's murdered her and hidden the body in a laundry basket?'

'Don't be ridiculous, Carla,' snapped Imogen, the stress of the last two days bubbling to the surface. 'That kind of talk is really unhelpful.'

'So what if she doesn't turn up? What's left to sort out for the wedding on Sunday?'

'Thankfully, now that the cakes and the wedding favours are done, there's only the flowers to chase up and Mum's already one step ahead. When she got back to the hotel yesterday afternoon she found the details of the supplier and confirmed that everything was on course for delivery on Saturday evening. Despite Karen's initial reservations, Brad has turned out to be a complete angel. He's not only running Mum up and down the hill in his hire car but also keeping her from having a total meltdown.'

Imogen poured herself a glass of home-made lime spritzer, added a scoop of ice and swallowed it down in one gulp.

'Alex and I had a meeting with Jerome last night and he assured us that he has everything under control. I'm sure we can manage to choreograph a wedding ceremony. There are thirty-six guests, and me and Alex – how hard can it be? When Dad was alive, he and Mum used to throw summer parties in the back garden for more than that!'

'Of course, Immie. We can totally do this without Fleur. You can rely on us!' declared Carla before turning her attention back to Millie to resume her earlier interrogation. 'So, Millie, who's going to be your escort to the evening reception?'

'Okay,' said Ella. 'We'd better get started. We've got a very busy schedule today if we want to finish decorating the wedding cake and finalising the wedding favours.'

'Oh, I'm so excited. You know, Ella, I actually think I like this chocolate one better than the one we lost in the fire.'

Imogen trotted off in Ella's wake to assist in the construction of her three-tiered chocolate extravaganza that would be the centrepiece of the top table on their wedding day.

'And we get to decorate our cake pops!' said Harriet, snatching up an apron to cover her pristine white linen tunic that Millie knew had cost more than she made in a month. 'Which shall we start with?'

'Mmm?' murmured Millie when she realised the silence meant Harriet was waiting for a response from her. The echo of Zach's telephone call with Chloe had stayed with her, pulling a knot ever tighter in her stomach and causing her to lose the thread of her explanations.

'Are you okay, Millie? Has something happened to upset you? It's just that you look like you spent the night in the village morgue. Why don't we have a coffee outside on the veranda before we start?'

'Oh, no, sorry. I'm fine, really. Right, we should start with the goldfish, the owl and the shark we moulded yesterday as practice before we move on to decorate the bride and the groom combos.'

Millie switched into professional chef mode – the go-to setting for when life tossed random grenades in her path. It's what she had done after the Luke fiasco when she had felt like she had landed on an alien planet – that everyone and everything around her had changed. Baking,

baking, baking until she dropped had saved her from chasing imaginary monsters down blind alleyways until she was clutching at her sanity with her fingernails. She secured her apron strings, brushed aside her worries and resolved to occupy her hands and her mind with culinary activities.

She removed the five trays of shaped cake pops from the freezer and set about preparing the candy melts she and Ella had sourced in Castries the previous week which, when softened, would form the outer shell of the cake pop wedding favours. She emptied the packets of different coloured chocolate buttons into individual bowls so she could dissolve them in the microwave before adding a dribble of vegetable oil.

'So, you hold the end of the stick and dip the cake into the melt like this.'

Millie demonstrated the action required to coat the cake pop that she had moulded into a passable goldfish shape with the bright orange candy melt, twirling it gently then removing it and setting it to cool in a block of polystyrene.

'Wow! Gracie would absolutely love this activity! Look Millie, what do you think? Shall we add a few of these for the guests with a sense of humour?' Carla held up the shark she had coated in a vivid purple-blue melt.

'I think we should stick to the brief,' interrupted Imogen from where she was piping buttercream onto one of the practice cakes. 'Any diversions and Mum will have a coronary.'

Carla rolled her eyes. 'Spoilsport!'

'My turn!' said Harriet. She selected the owl she had made the previous day and dipped it into the pink dish, twisting it as Millie had demonstrated, giggling with pleasure. 'I love this! It's like a baking class and an art class all rolled into one. Can we paint them now, Millie?'

'We need to pop them into the freezer to harden whilst we get on with making the wedding favours.'

Millie coached Carla and Harriet in how to coat the balls of chocolate cake with either white chocolate for the bride or dark chocolate for the groom. When they had finished all thirty-six, they were whisked into the freezer and the earlier 'test' cake pops were removed. With paintbrushes and mini pots of food colouring, Millie showed them how to paint on the goldfish's eyes and the white and black Nemo stripes.

Carla gave her shark a huge set of teeth. 'No prizes for its inspiration!'

'It's certainly got Greg's eyebrows!' laughed Harriet, painting huge white eyes on her owl and highlighting the contours of its chest feathers in black.

Once again it was almost six o'clock by the time the women took a break to assess their progress. Imogen and Alex's wedding cake was finished. It looked amazing: each of the three tiers covered in swirls of buttercream and scattered with hand-crafted flowers, chocolate hearts, butterflies and double clefs in a nod to the band Alex played guitar in when he had time. Fearful of another disaster, Imogen had turned down Ella's offer to take it back to the hotel with them that evening, insisting that she would ask one of the men to drive over to collect it on the Sunday morning before the ceremony.

However, the stars of the show were most definitely the cake pops. The bride version had been dipped in white chocolate and sported a tiara of tiny edible pearls and white lace decoration for the wedding dress. The groom had been given a splendid top hat painted in black food colouring and even had a tiny waistcoat etched on his chest along with a miniature pink bow tie to match the bride's bouquet. The unique wedding favours were stored in the freezer and would be wrapped in cellophane and tied with colour-co-ordinated ribbons ready to be given pride of place on the tables in the wedding marquee.

Millie was exhausted. Her face muscles ached from the charade of excitement she had been forced to enact all day when all she could think about was what was happening with Zach and Chloe. Only Ella, and perhaps Imogen, who kept sending her worried looks, suspected that something was amiss, but neither of them dared to ask in case they upset her further. She was thankful for their discretion.

In fact, once again she found herself grateful for her obsession with all things culinary that had come to her rescue when her world had tipped on its axis. She knew she could count on her cakes to rise, her panna cotta to set, her soufflés to rise. She could predict which mix of spices would meld into a sensation on the lips, which liqueur would enhance which fruit compote, and what herbs to use with which meats. What she would never be able to understand, no matter how much effort she put into it, was how the male mind worked.

From now on, she wasn't even going to try.

Chapter Eleven

After Imogen and her bridesmaids had left, Millie couldn't face making a start on the tidying up. One thing she knew for certain was that Zach would not be appearing at the French doors, the usual smirk on his face and a sarcastic comment on his lips about her propensity for scattering culinary chaos. Ignoring everything she had been taught at college, and all the encouragement from her super-organised sister Jen, she decided to leave the clearing up until the next morning.

She locked the French doors and took a moment to drink in the view from the veranda. The Pitons seemed to reflect her mood perfectly: dark, glowering pyramids of shadow setting sail in the inky black of the Caribbean Sea. The town of Soufrière slumbered peacefully at their base, amber street lights twinkling like dancing fairies. She glanced down at the swimming pool, the rectangle of turquoise somehow drawing her towards its depths.

On impulse, she kicked off her sandals, dropped her straw bag on one of the sun loungers and skipped down the wooden steps to the terrace. Without allowing herself the time to talk herself out of it, she stripped off her capri trousers and Breton T-shirt and launched into the pool. The cool water felt like a veil of silk slipping over her skin and she powered through twenty laps without stopping until her breath came out in spurts but her mind was clear and refreshed.

So what if Zach was probably, at that very moment, entertaining his ex-girlfriend in his little wooden cabin amidst the cocoa trees whilst Binks snoozed outside on the decking. It was not as though they had been an item, just friends.

But Millie knew that no matter how many times she reminded herself of that fact, she was deceiving herself. The way her heart bounced with joy when-ever Zach arrived on the veranda, or gave her that quirky, sardonic smile, she knew her feelings for him stretched well beyond friendship, despite the short time she had known him. She knew that her sister had met and fallen in love with her husband, Oscar, whilst visiting their mother in Provence. He had been on a backpacking holiday and had moved on after only two weeks, but Jen knew she was going to spend the rest of her life with him. And so she had – one country village wedding and two children later they were happier than ever.

When she had asked Jen how she had known Oscar was her soulmate so quickly she had simply responded that she just knew, that it wasn't something she could put into words. It was a feeling of absolute certainty that they were on the same wavelength and the fact that she couldn't bear the thought of being apart from him even for a second. Millie had taken those pearls of sisterly wisdom on board and had waited for those feelings to sneak up on her when she met Luke, but they hadn't. In fact, looking back, she had often craved an afternoon of solitude, but she put that down to them working together in the restaurant.

For the first time that day, Millie felt a smile stretch her lips as she thought of her sister and an overwhelming urge to hear her voice descended. She pulled herself out of the swimming pool, grabbed her clothes and jogged back to her studio above the garage. She snatched up a sunflower-yellow beach kaftan she had bought at Anisha's shop in Soufrière, grabbed a beer from the fridge, then settled on the little balcony overlooking the courtyard and took out her phone.

'Jen? Hi, it's Millie.'

'Hi, Millie, it's great to hear from you, but do you know what time it is here in Oxford?'

'Oh, no! I'm so sorry, I completely forgot about the time difference.'

'It's okay,' laughed Jen. 'Don't worry I wasn't asleep. I was just giving the kitchen a last wipe down before Lily's party tomorrow.'

Millie shoved the image of her own kitchen into the deep, dark crevices of her mind. How could she share the same genes with her sister yet be so completely different when it came to organisational skills and tidiness. She knew that her niece's fifth birthday party the next day would have been planned down to the very last colour-co-ordinated detail, with nothing left to chance. There would even be a selection of delicious home-baked alternatives for the guests who had allergies or parents with an aversion to sugar.

'Ah, Jen, I'm so sorry to be missing Lily's party. Will you give her a huge hug from me and tell her that there's something special for her in the post? Has Mum arrived safely?'

'Yes. I picked her up from the airport yesterday. I'm not sure whether I should wait until you get home to tell you…'

'Tell me what?' Millie snapped, the familiar tightening of panic invading her chest as she thought of anything happening to her beloved mum, Monique. After the unexpected loss of her father two years ago, her mother had returned to the village in Provence where she grew up to take the local community by storm, quickly making a name for herself with her G&T soirées and her penchant for Latin ballroom dancing. If anything was to happen to her… but to her relief, her sister was laughing.

'Remember I told you that her friend Solange from salsa class got her navel pierced last month?'

'Oh my God! Don't tell me Mum's gone and…'

'No, no, no.'

'Then what?'

'Are you sitting down?' Jen giggled, enjoying keeping Millie in suspense.

'Jen…'

'She got a tattoo!'

'A tattoo? Are you winding me up? Mum got a tattoo? What sort of tattoo?'

'It's actually quite tasteful. In fact, I'm thinking of getting one myself.'

Millie rolled her eyes. She picked up her beer and took a sip. What was happening to her family? But then another thought occurred to her. Maybe it was her — maybe she had become a boring old stick-in-the-mud, unwilling to venture out of her comfort zone in case disaster was waiting around the corner to claim its next victim. Suddenly she experienced a lightbulb moment. That was exactly what Zach had been trying to get her to understand. That there was a huge, wide world out there to explore, to experience, to enjoy and she should grasp the opportunity to throw herself into every new adventure whenever she could. After all, without Zach's encouragement, when would she have ever attempted a zip wire ride?

'Millie? Millie? Are you still there?'

'Yes, I'm still here. How was the Cornwall Living Show?'

'Oh, yes, that was great fun, but what I want to know is how's the Paradise Cookery School? Are you enjoying presenting the classes? What are the students like? I've spoken to Claudia a couple of times this week and she told me that you've had to divert from the Chocolate and Confetti itinerary. What an awful thing to happen.'

Millie smiled to herself. Jen was a seasoned expert in presenting cookery classes, whether to her pupils at the local primary school, to the new students at catering college or to a gathering of her local WI members. However, as a detail obsessive, she didn't cope well with any last-minute amendments to her carefully organised schedules.

Whereas Millie, on the other hand, was so used to things going pear-shaped because of her chaotic approach to orderliness that she had developed the skills needed to compromise and make it look like that was intended all along – just like she had been able to do during the last two days. Yes, she might still have issues with her self-confidence after what had happened with Luke, but one thing she knew for certain was that she could cook, and bake, and decorate cake pops!

'Ella and I have everything under control. Imogen's wedding cake is finished and it looks amazing.'

'I know. Claudia forwarded me the email Ella sent her with the photographs attached. Was it chocolate sponge?'

'Yes. Did she send you the photos of the cake pops me, Carla and Harriet made to replace the wedding favours that were also damaged in the fire?'

'No! Wow, what a fabulous idea! You are a brilliant cake designer, Millie. Oh, I just knew this adventure in the Caribbean would be exactly what you needed. So, enough about the cookery classes, what I want to hear is all the gossip about a guy called Zach that Ella just happened to mention in passing. Have you taken your big sister's advice about indulging in a little romance over there on that paradise island?'

Millie felt her heart give a sharp nip. If Jen had asked her that question yesterday, she would have delivered a completely different answer. As it was, the last thing she wanted to gossip with her sister about was Zach Barker.

'Sorry to disappoint you, but there's nothing to report.'

'Really? That isn't what Ella said. She told Claudia that you had gone off for a day exploring the rainforest together. Come on, Millie, spill the details to your old married sister. Oscar's idea of romance is taking me to the village cricket match to make the teas! Tell me about Zach. He's Claudia and Tim's estate manager, isn't he?'

'Yes, he's on secondment from Claudia's manor house in the Cotswolds where she has her cookery school. I'm surprised you didn't meet him when you were over there presenting that course for Claudia last Christmas. It's true, he has shown me some of the island whilst I've been here, but we're just friends, Jen. Nothing else.' Millie heard a deep intake of breath and knew she was about to be on the receiving end of a lecture about moving on from Luke and that enjoying a holiday fling with no strings attached was the best therapy for the broken-hearted, so she added, 'Actually, his girlfriend has just arrived from the UK, so I don't think I'll be seeing much of him before I fly back home on Monday.'

'Shame,' giggled Jen. 'I checked out his Facebook page and he's hot!'

Millie felt a dart of regret shoot through her. Wasn't that exactly what her first impression had been of Zach Barker? Along with his infuriating sarcasm and ability to materialise whenever there was a chance to witness Millie at her least elegant?

'There must be plenty of other handsome guys on holiday in St Lucia. Doesn't Ella have a son? Isn't he a journalist on the local newspaper? Does *he* have a girlfriend?'

'Jen…'

'All I'm saying is you can't go through life without taking a chance on love. I won't let you do that. Lily and Sofia do not want to visit an ageing spinster aunt who spends all her time knitting and sewing and rustling up the odd Victoria sponge, ruing the time that has passed her by.'

Millie had no intention of satisfying her sister's demands by telling her about the date Lottie had arranged for her the previous week with Marc, one of the waiters at the Purple Parrot where she worked. She wasn't sure which bit of juicy information her sister would enjoy the most; the fact that Marc had left to use the bathroom facilities and not returned, or the fact that he had subsequently been arrested for his part in a drug-running operation. If she hadn't been put off dating by the fiasco with Luke before that, then she most certainly had been when she had learned about Marc's fate from Lottie. She was now a fully paid-up member of the Love Cynic Club.

'Jen, I'm here to work! You might think all I've got to do is lie around all day on a sun lounger, sipping cocktails and soaking up the sunshine, but actually I'm spending every single minute shopping for ingredients, testing and tweaking recipes, not to mention the terrifying task of delivering a bespoke cookery course to the standards required by a celebrity TV chef. If you want to know the truth I'm absolutely exhausted.'

'You're holding back on something, Millie, I can tell from your voice. I understand if you don't want to share whatever it is over the phone, but I'm coming down to London as soon as you get back. I'll treat you to afternoon tea at Fortnum's and we can have a girly heart-to-heart. Won't take no for an answer.'

Millie chatted to Jen for a few more minutes, asking about Sofia's swimming lessons and Lily's birthday cake which, predictably, had a ballerina theme. She had loved reconnecting across the miles, but she didn't feel any better than she had before she had called. In fact, she could now add a large dollop of homesickness to her expanding list of ailments.

'Okay, I'd better let you get to bed or you'll be too tired to control the happy hordes tomorrow. Send my love to Mum, and to Oscar and the girls.'

'I will. Love you, Millie.'

'You too.'

Millie sat back in her chair, tipped her chin upwards and stared at the sky. After a few seconds of contemplation, she was sure she saw a shooting star amongst the millions of others scattered across the inky blue canopy overhead. She quickly made a wish, but watching the cosmic spectacle from a seat in the Grand Circle alone didn't offer the same pleasure as it would have if there had been someone to share it with. Jen was right. Life was better when there was someone special by your side.

A heavy mantle of fatigue descended. It had been a long and stressful day, and even though it was barely nine o'clock she decided that in her current mood of melancholy there was nothing else to do but to curl up in bed and partake in a bout of self-indulgent weeping.

Chapter Twelve

Millie woke early and for a few blissful seconds she wallowed in the luxury of the morning's birdsong. The sun bleached through the muslin curtains and from the slice of pale blue between the drapes she could see it was going to be another blissful day in paradise. Then reality hit and she groaned out loud. Why had she thought it was a good idea to leave the clearing up until today?

She leapt out of bed and straight into the shower to blast away the cobwebs. She was relieved to see it was only six-thirty so she had plenty of time to erase the evidence of the previous day's culinary exploits.

She wasn't entirely sure whether Imogen and her friends would be coming over to the Paradise Cookery School that day – what would have been, in normal circumstances, the final day of Claudia's Chocolate & Confetti course. When they had left in their hire car the previous day she had simply left the choice up to them, assuring Imogen that she and Ella would be there from ten o'clock onwards. They could either have a full day's tuition on making chocolate eclairs and profiteroles as per the original itinerary Claudia had planned or they could make a mountain of cupcakes and decorate them with a variety of exotic toppings – an activity that Gracie could join in with. Or, if they all had better things to do, like organising the whole wedding ceremony singlehandedly because of the situation with the disappearing wedding planner, and preferred to give the last day a miss, then that was fine too.

Millie had to admit she was disappointed the course hadn't run as smoothly as she had hoped but, thankfully, that had nothing to do with her or Ella's organisational skills. She knew Julia had emailed Claudia to personally apologise for what had happened. Claudia had immediately offered to refund the course fee but Julia wouldn't hear of it, singing Millie and Ella's praises as not only fantastic pastry chefs and course presenters, but awesome human beings for coming to their rescue with the replacement wedding cake and creating the favours.

Millie checked her phone but there were no messages. She refused to admit to herself that what she was secretly hoping for was a text from Zach explaining exactly what had happened the previous day when he had been summoned to the airport to collect Chloe. Did his lack of contact mean that they had resumed their relationship? Or had he simply met Chloe in order to reiterate his assertion that he wasn't interested in getting engaged – the reason Chloe had terminated their relationship in the first place. Millie was totally confused at her sudden reappearance, especially as the last thing Zach had told her about Chloe was that he had heard through the grapevine that she was engaged. So what was going on?

Millie heaved a sigh and slid her toes into her sparkly flip-flops. If she thought about the Zach and Chloe situation any longer there was a risk her head might explode, so she prescribed herself a morning of scrubbing the kitchen floor and work-stations as therapy for her dalliance with confusion. She flicked on the radio and, with the reggae rhythms to aid progress, she was finished by eight o'clock.

She ground a handful of roasted coffee beans, made herself a cafetière of the best coffee in the world, and took her mug out onto the veranda. Three more days to enjoy the wonderful view, the tranquillity of the villa and its grounds, and the friendships she had made during three weeks' sabbatical from her job at the little patisserie in Hammersmith. She stared at the scene in front of her, trying to fix every tiny detail in her mind's eye so she would be able to conjure up the image on those drab, grey, drizzle-soaked days that London was so apt to produce.

She must have nodded off because the next thing she knew a warm tongue was caressing her fingers and she was woken by an enthusiastic bark of welcome.

'Oh, hi, Binks!' Millie smiled at the spaniel's friendly face, her heart performing a swift somersault in anticipation of seeing Zach. But there was no sign of him. 'How did you get…?'

'Binks? Binks? Come back here!'

Millie peered over the balcony onto the poolside terrace below the veranda where a woman was patting her knees in an attempt to persuade Binks to return to heel, but he simply stood on the top step, his tongue hanging from his mouth, and ignored her. As tall and willowy as a supermodel, Binks's new friend shielded her eyes and noticed Millie for the first time.

'Oh, I'm so sorry for intruding. Is Binks disturbing you?'

'Not at all. He's very welcome here. I think he wants a drink, though.'

Millie jumped up from her seat and surreptitiously ran her eyes over her visitor before disappearing into the kitchen to fetch a bowl of water for Binks.

'Can I offer you a coffee?' she called over her shoulder. 'I've just made a fresh cafetière.'

'I'd love one, thanks. I'm Chloe, by the way.'

'Hello, Chloe. I'm Amelia.'

Millie paused for a few seconds whilst pouring the milk into a china jug. She *never* introduced herself as Amelia, always Millie, but for some reason she had felt the necessity to use her Sunday name in the presence of Zach's, well… was she his ex-girlfriend or current partner, or maybe even his fiancée?

'Ah, yes, you're the cook, aren't you?' Chloe sniffed before slumping down into the chair Millie had just vacated and arranging her diaphanous scarlet sundress into perfect folds around her knees. Her appearance was so polished that she could have graced a glamorous photoshoot without any retouching. Every inch of her skin had been professionally bronzed and her short auburn hair had been carefully teased into random waves to give it that 'just-tumbled-out-of-bed' look. Millie wondered if that was true. Had Chloe just left Zach snoozing in his wooden lodge to take Binks for a quick walk? But Zach was an early riser, so did that mean that…

A spasm of something Millie didn't want to label shot through her veins. She quickly shoved the disturbing emotion to one side and plastered a smile on her face when she handed Chloe her coffee and took a seat across the table from her.

'I am a cook, yes. But I actually prefer the term chef, although my current job title is cookery course presenter here at the Paradise Cookery School. No doubt Zach told you about Claudia's horse-riding accident?'

'Oh yes, Zach tells me everything.'

Chloe smiled but the gesture didn't reach her jade green eyes that had been highlighted with gold eyeliner and the longest false eyelashes Millie had seen. She noticed that whilst Chloe fidgeted with the handle of her coffee cup, she resolutely refused to raise it to her lips. As the initial shock of meeting Chloe receded, a wave of curiosity rolled over Millie. Whilst she was by no means an expert in the interpretation of body language, it was clear to even the most casual onlooker that her visitor was agitated. Millie wondered when she would get around to spitting out what she had obviously made a special trip to say.

'I thought I'd let Zach have a lie in this morning. He's been working far too hard since he arrived in St Lucia. Is it true that he had to help you tidy up and *clean* the kitchen after one of your cookery sessions?'

'Well…'

'You know that's not his job, don't you? This is a huge plantation to manage, never mind the fact that he's had to organise and lead the quad bike safari and the treasure hunt – that's a lot for one guy. Anyway, now I'm here, he won't have any time to help you out. When are you leaving for the UK?'

Millie was taken aback by the directness of Chloe's conversation. She was being made to feel like a naughty schoolgirl who had taken up too much of her teacher's time with her antics and was now being told in no uncertain terms that from now on she would have to fend for herself. She shifted uncomfortably in her seat. She didn't want to appear rude, but she wasn't about to let Chloe believe that it had been her, or Ella, who had been the instigator of Zach's invaluable assistance in the kitchen.

'Actually, I think if you ask Zach, he'll tell you that there was no coercion involved. He very kindly *offered* to help Ella and I with the clearing up after a very hectic day in the cookery school because of a dreadful incident at the hotel where Imogen's wonderful wedding cake was destroyed by a fire…'

'That's not Zach's fault, though, is it? And if you're so busy, how have you found the time for a jaunt to Castries market and wherever else you've been? I had to wait ages for Zach to collect me from the airport because he was busy being your tour guide.'

'Again, I think you need to have a conversation with Zach about that.'

Millie was about to continue with a self-justifying explanation that on each and every occasion she had been on a trip with Zach, whether it was for a drink at the Purple Parrot, a hike up the Pitons, or a very pleasurable sojourn in the tiny wooden cabin during the daily burst of liquid sunshine, the excursions had been at Zach's instigation, not hers – especially the zip wire flight at Treetops Adventures! However, it struck her that she had no need to explain anything to Chloe, who had clearly only turned up on her veranda that morning to wrangle information out of her about Zach's movements whilst he'd been in the Caribbean and she had no intention of playing that game.

The air between them crackled with discomfort until Binks returned from drinking his fill and gave Millie's hand an affection lick of thanks.

'You seem to be rather familiar with Binks?'

Millie smiled at Zach's faithful canine companion, running her fingers over his smooth coat. 'I think it's because he knows there's always a treat to be found here.'

'You do know that baked goods are bad for dogs, don't you?'

'Of course, I…'

'And humans, for that matter.' Chloe patted her flat stomach before casting a critical eye over Millie's contours.

The thoroughness of the unexpected scrutiny caused a flare of indignation to ignite inside Millie. Whilst she was a perfectly normal weight, she certainly wasn't as slender as Chloe, which, coupled with her height, actually made her look a little on the gaunt side. She opened her mouth to respond, but Chloe must have noticed the look of incredulity on Millie's face at the overtly personal comment, because she sensibly decided to switch tack.

'It's really beautiful here, isn't it?'

'Yes, it is…'

'I'm so pleased Zach and I are able to have this time together. I'm not sure whether he mentioned that we broke up briefly a few weeks ago, but now we're back together it's as though we're enjoying an early honeymoon.'

'A honeymoon?' Millie spluttered before she could stop herself.

Chloe laughed, a high tinkling false sound. 'Well, not exactly, but who knows what will happen in such a tropical paradise? Love amongst the palm trees? Eh? Anyway, I must be making tracks. Zach will be wondering where I am and he doesn't like to be kept waiting. We're planning a romantic boat trip to Martinique today. Have you been?'

'No, as I said, I haven't had much time to sightsee. I'm not on holiday!'

'Oh well. Good luck with the baking.'

Chloe called Binks to heel and he obediently trotted off in her wake as she made her way to the end of the veranda, the ribbons of her sunhat rippling in the breeze like the tails of a kite. She walked as though she was on a catwalk, swinging her hips but keeping her head high and still.

Millie opened her mouth to call goodbye but quickly closed it again. She had been left in no doubt whatsoever that she had just been well and truly warned off from fraternising with the hunky cocoa plantation manager, Zach Barker. Despite her acute sense of loss of their blossoming friend-ship, Millie found her lips twitch upwards. She would bet her favourite handbag that Chloe would never in a million years have ended up rolling in a ditch with Zach or have agreed to swap her Louboutins for Skechers to channel her inner Tinkerbell on an exhilarating journey through the tropical foliage.

A chuckle erupted from her throat, followed by a deep belly laugh that Ella would be proud of. She laughed and laughed until tears trickled down her cheeks. She had no idea what Chloe did for a living, but if she were an actress she would have been awarded the wooden spoon in the contest for the 'most transparent attempt to warn off a love rival'. She would have had more respect for the woman if she had screamed from the poolside 'hands off my man, you harlot!' and ran away.

She wondered what Zach saw in Chloe. In contrast to his girlfriend, he was nothing if not straightforward and honest to the point of rudeness. And why had he changed his mind so quickly about resuming their relationship? But Millie knew she was the last person to ask for answers when it came to the task of unravelling the mysteries of romance.

Chapter Thirteen

It was true what they said. A good laugh is the best medicine for an aching heart. When Millie dried her eyes on a piece of kitchen towel, her spirits had ascended a couple of notches up the happiness scale. She carried her empty mug and Chloe's untouched coffee into the kitchen, rinsed them in the sink and put them back in the cupboard. Perhaps Zach's obsessive neatness was starting to rub off on her at last.

She checked her watch. Nine o'clock. She wondered what the day would have in store. She was expecting Ella to arrive at nine-thirty but she still hadn't heard anything from Imogen or Julia so had no idea whether she would have any students interested in learning how to make choux pastry. She decided that if no one turned up, she would suggest to Ella that they took a trip down to Soufrière to see how Lottie was getting on in her managerial role at the Purple Parrot.

'Morning, Millie. Isn't it another wonderful day?' chirped Ella as she hooked the handles of her huge canvas bag over her shoulder so she could wave goodbye to Henri, who had dropped her off in the courtyard with a farewell toot to Millie.

'Mmm,' said Millie, her tone non-commital.

'Okay, before we go any further, I want you to tell me what's going on. And don't say "nothing, I'm fine" because I've been a mother for twenty-eight years and I've heard every avoidance tactic in the book so I know when something's festering.'

Ella plonked her well-padded bottom into the cane chair next to Millie, folded her arms over her voluminous Kermit-green kaftan, and levelled her gaze at Millie, her lips pursed in expectation.

Millie scanned her brain for a suitable alternate scenario that didn't feature Zach in the lead role, and which would satisfy Ella's line of questioning but came up with a blank. She opened her mouth to speak but no words issued forth, so she closed it before opening it again.

'Don't just sit there like a gobsmacked goldfish. Speak up. It's Zach, isn't it? I noticed he was some-what conspicuous by his absence yesterday. What's happened? Have you had a falling out?'

'Not as such.'

'So what is it?'

'His girlfriend has arrived from the UK.'

'His girlfriend? Are you sure, dear? I would have thought that if Zach had a girlfriend we would have heard all about her. Perhaps you're mistaken. Maybe his visitor is his sister.'

'Zach doesn't have a sister. It's Chloe, his ex. Don't look at me like that. She called round here an hour ago on the pretext of an early morning walk with Binks but it was really so she could make it quite clear that she was with Zach and I should keep my hands off her man.' Millie grimaced when she thought of the encounter.

'A little melodramatic, don't you think?'

'Chloe has nothing to worry about. Zach and I are just friends. But, Ella, I have to admit that it was a shock when she arrived out of the blue and demanded that Zach collect her from the airport. We'd just had the most fabulous time zip lining through the rainforest yesterday morning. I thought… well, I thought we had a connection, something I had never felt with Luke. When I'm with Zach he makes me feel as if I can do anything, that I can conquer my worst fears — and enjoy myself while I'm doing it.'

Millie allowed her lips to turn upwards, her go-to expression when she recalled their adventure flying through the tropical treetops like a pair of carefree monkeys.

'I'm certain that Zach is still your friend, Millie.'

'So why hasn't he contacted me since Chloe arrived? He sped off to the airport and I haven't heard from him since. Friends don't do that. No, it looks like he and Chloe have reconciled and she's here in St Lucia to have a good time and wants him all to herself.'

Millie fiddled with the friendship bracelet Lottie had made for her the previous week and experienced a sudden urge to weep. Would it always be the same outcome for her whenever she made a tentative foray into the dating jungle? It seemed that every time she cracked open a tiny chink in her armour, disaster managed to wheedle its way in and blast her heart apart.

'Okay, it looks like someone needs cheering up.' Ella pushed herself out of her chair and meandered into the kitchen. 'And what is the best treatment for a bout of melancholy?'

Millie stared at Ella. She had known the Caribbean chef for less than three weeks, but she felt as though she was an old friend. Someone who knew her from the inside out, not the other way around. Her spirits shot up another notch. She only had a few days left in this wonderful island paradise and it would be a tragedy to spend them moping over something that had never happened. If, in the very unlikely event that she and Zach *had* got together, it was only going to be a holiday fling at best, and whilst that would have pleased her sister no end, it was not what *she* needed at all. Actually, she thought to herself as she followed Ella into the kitchen, she had probably had a narrow escape from falling head first into yet another relationship calamity.

'Well, in my book, the best medicine for sadness is a session of baking.'

'Exactly – so let's gets started!' beamed Ella, tying her aprons strings securely and reaching for the ingredients she needed for a morning at the coalface of culinary labour. 'Have you heard anything from Julia?'

'Not yet.' Millie reached into her pocket to check her phone. 'Hang on. Here's a text from Imogen. It must have just arrived.' She scrolled through the missive quickly. 'Ah, they're not coming today. Too much to organise for the wedding on Sunday. I'm not surprised.'

'That poor girl,' sighed Ella, sifting flour into a bowl. 'She must be ruing the day she decided to get married abroad.'

'It was Julia's idea. Imogen and Alex wanted to have their wedding ceremony at the local parish church followed by a marquee in the garden for their reception.'

'Right, then – if the Paradise Cookery School is closed for business this beautiful Friday morning, then we're going to bake a few batches of cupcakes and take them down to Lottie at the Purple Parrot. We deserve a break.'

'Sounds like a plan,' smiled Millie, already starting to feel better as she assembled the ingredients and started to separate the polka dot bun cases into the baking trays. 'Why don't we double up the mixture and deliver a box of cupcakes to the hotel afterwards as a treat for Imogen and her wedding party? I feel so sorry for her – and Julia.'

'A wonderful idea, Millie.'

A gentle ripple of calypso music added to the relaxed ambience in the kitchen and within the hour they had amassed five dozen cupcakes, decorated in a variety of frostings from ginger and lime, to pineapple and coconut, and chocolate chip and orange zest. Millie was particularly proud of the lemon drizzle cupcakes she had made from the lemons she had harvested herself from the trees next to the pool.

Ella packed the cupcakes up into two huge Tupperware boxes — one destined for Lottie at the Purple Parrot and the other one for Imogen at the hotel — and called for a taxi to take them down the hill to Soufrière. Inevitably, her friend Clavie was sent to collect them. His vehicle was so ancient that it steadfastly refused to navigate the steep incline up to the villa and he told them he would meet them at the bottom of the driveway in twenty minutes.

'Ready?' asked Millie, ditching a handful of utensils in the already jam-packed sink and casting her cocoa-splodged apron into the mix.

Ella rolled her eyes as she carefully folded her still-pristine apron and slotted it back in the kitchen drawer. She hooked her arm around one of the plastic containers and handed the remaining one to Millie.

'Ready.'

Together they trotted down the driveway, chatting companionably about ideas for new recipes until Ella stopped suddenly and peered into the foliage to her left. Millie squinted in the same direction and could just about make out a dark silhouette lurking amongst the cocoa palms. As her vision grew accustomed to the gloom between the trees, she realised that it wasn't one person, but in fact a couple. The woman had her spine pressed against one of the trunks and the man was leaning towards her in an intimate pose, their faces mere inches apart.

An explosion of recognition burst into Millie's brain and her heart squeezed painfully. It was Zach and Chloe. She felt Ella's hand on her arm gently urging her onwards as Clavie was waiting for them at the bottom of the hill, but she couldn't drag her eyes away from the scene. Until that moment, she knew she had harboured a smidgeon of optimism that Zach would have reaffirmed his decision that he did not want a permanent relationship with Chloe, but now that hope had been extinguished.

Fortunately, neither Zach nor Chloe had noticed their presence – obviously too wrapped up in each other to allow the outside world to intrude on their bubble of romance. Millie hadn't realised she had been holding her breath and gulped in a lungful of oxygen, yet she still felt lightheaded. She smiled weakly at the sympathy she saw reflected in Ella's chocolate brown eyes and followed her mutely to the taxi for their ride down to Soufrière.

Chapter Fourteen

'Hi, Lottie,' called Ella trotting into the kitchen of the Purple Parrot and depositing the cupcakes on the bench.

'Wow! Ella. These look amazing. Thank you. Hi, Millie. How are things up at the Paradise Cookery School? Have the chocoholics had their fix?'

Lottie pulled Millie into a warm, jasmine-infused hug before leading her and Ella out to a table on the bleached wooden decking over-looking the beach and the sparkling Caribbean Sea beyond. The majestic Pitons presided over the whole scene, which looked like something straight from a film set due to the presence of a multi-sailed galleon at anchor in the bay which had just disgorged its passengers into the streets of Soufrière for a morning of shopping and sampling the local cuisine.

The Purple Parrot was busy with diners but Lottie sat down next to Millie and signalled for

Travis behind the bar to bring them some drinks. Now that Millie was relaxing in a comfortable seat, enjoying the myriad boats bobbing about on the ocean, she was able to put the scene with Zach and Chloe out of her mind and concentrate on enjoying her first full day's break from her duties at the Paradise Cookery School since she had arrived on St Lucia.

'It's been a strange week, to be honest,' Millie told Lottie as Ella unpacked the cupcakes onto one of Claudia's china plates and they all reached for their favourite.

'Hello everyone,' beamed Travis, Soufrière's answer to Damien Hirst currently moonlighting as a waiter, as he set down three goldfish bowl-sized glasses filled to the sugared rim with a lurid green liquid that looked like pureed grass. 'Okay, so today, especially for my three favourite women, I have the pleasure of presenting you with… a trio of Purple Parrot cocktails with a Travisesque twist!'

If Millie didn't already know that Travis usually made his living in Soufrière as an artist, she would never have guessed he had a creative bone in his body when she saw the car crash cocktail that had been placed on the table in front of her. The glass had been stuffed with miniature umbrellas and twizzle sticks and finished with a sprig of frosted mint. She prayed that it would taste better than it looked.

'Thanks, Travis.'

'Hey, no problem, man. Enjoy.' And he sauntered off to chat to a pair of Scandinavian teenagers who were making it abundantly clear that they would like nothing more than to help Travis shake his cocktails.

Millie decided to throw caution to the wind and chance a sip. She wasn't in the habit of indulging in spirit-based drinks at eleven o'clock in the morning, but she was in the Caribbean and now that her services were no longer needed at the Paradise Cookery School, why shouldn't she relax a little?

'Mmm, that's absolutely amazing!' Far from being the grass-flavoured sludge Millie had been expecting, the ice-cold, mint-infused cocktail smashed into her taste buds and sent tingles cascading down her throat.

'Don't look so surprised!' giggled Lottie, flicking her long magenta hair over her shoulder, causing the silver necklaces at her throat to glisten in the sun. 'Me, Anisha and Travis have spent all week devising and tasting a whole new menu of signature cocktails for the Purple Parrot. It was tough work, but someone had to do it! Well, we couldn't exactly continue offering *Andy's Blasts*, could we?'

'And nor should you!' exclaimed Ella, having tasted the cocktail and shoved it away in disgust. 'That man, and so many others like him, are a menace to our communities. They prey on the vulnerable for their own financial gain and I, for one, will not stand by and let them get away with it. I shall be contacting the authorities to make sure that Andrew O'Leary is given the stiffest of penalties when his case eventually gets to court.'

When the Purple Parrot's erstwhile proprietor had been arrested for his part in a drug-smuggling incident, Lottie had been presented with a decision to either close the popular restaurant-cum-bar at one of the busiest times of the year or step up to the challenge of managing the restaurant with the help of friends. Like everyone who was part of the St Lucian community, she didn't have to wait long for the offers of help to come flooding in, and Travis and Anisha had taken over the jobs of barman and waitress respectively, enabling the Purple Parrot to continue offering fabulous food, made from the freshest of ingredients, and a long list of potent rum cocktails to the hungry and thirsty tourists who descended on Soufrière every day to access a little slice of paradise.

'I agree with you, Ella. I just wish he'd left his business in a better state,' sighed Lottie. 'There's a queue of creditors howling for their money and nothing in the till to pay them with. I had no idea it was so difficult to run a bar. Perhaps I should have let the police close it down until Andrew's future is decided.'

'No way! The Purple Parrot is an institution which can only go from strength to strength now that you are in charge!' beamed Ella, her expression reflecting her absolute confidence in Lottie's capabilities and securing a grateful smile from Soufrière's newest bar manager.

'Well, I don't know what I would do if Dylan, Travis and Anisha hadn't rallied round to help out. Hey, Millie, instead of flying home on Monday, why don't you stay on here in St Lucia? You can have a free rein in the kitchen, experiment with all the exotic ingredients you want?'

Millie glanced at Ella. She would have liked nothing more than to jump at the chance to run her own kitchen again, especially in the Caribbean, never mind spend more time with these wonderful people, friends she had grown to love and trust. And maybe she would have given Lottie's offer serious consideration had it been issued the previous day if it had meant that she could have continued her friendship with Zach, but that was no longer a possibility.

Whilst she wasn't looking forward to leaving St Lucia, she didn't have to be psychic to predict that the atmosphere around the villa would be uncomfortable if she was going to have to avoid taking her morning run around the estate for fear of coming into contact with Zach and Chloe. Anyway, Poppy would never forgive her if she abandoned her job at the patisserie.

'Thanks, Lottie. It's a very kind offer, and I am tempted, but I've already been here a week longer than Étienne agreed. If I don't go back to work next week, I'm not sure I'll have a job to go back to.'

'Life's not all about work, Millie.'

Millie couldn't stop herself from smiling when she saw the young girl's gaze slip towards the Dive Shack next door where the object of her affections was busy getting his boat ready for the next influx of enthusiastic divers. Dylan must have sensed their scrutiny because he straightened up and waved at them, his blond, surfer-dude hair sticking up as he grinned at Lottie.

'How's Dylan?'

'Fab!' Lottie's eyes sparkled. 'We've just got back from a trip to Castries market. Look what he bought me.' Lottie held out her hand for Millie to inspect the slender silver ring, set with a tiny turquoise stone. 'Oh, it's not an engagement ring or anything like that, but it doesn't matter. I love it!'

From Lottie's wide smile, it was clear to Millie that she loved the gift-giver even more. Her heart twisted with affection for the two lovebirds, who had sealed their partnership only a week ago when Dylan had discovered her boss had been using his boat for illicit purposes and Andrew's life had unravelled.

'Hey, hang on! It's Friday!'

'Yee…ees…' laughed Millie.

'So why are you and Ella here? I thought Chocolate and Confetti was a five-day course? Why aren't you up at the villa doing what you do best? Showcasing and tasting delicious chocolatey recipes?' Lottie screwed up her nose in confusion as she selected a strand of hair to coil between her fingers, the jumble of silver bangles jangling from her wrist to her elbow.

'As I said, it's a bit of a long story.' Millie proceeded to give Lottie a brief synopsis of the problems that had befallen Imogen and Alex's wedding arrangements.

'So is there still no news from the wedding planner?'

'No. It's as though she's disappeared off the face of the earth.'

'I bet she's just taken their cash and dashed,' declared Lottie, her kohl-ringed eyes wide with sympathy.

'You could be right, but then, why did Fleur meet up with Imogen and Alex when they arrived on Sunday to go through everything? Imogen said neither of them had any suspicions at all that she wouldn't come through with everything she'd promised them.'

'Oh, Imogen must be really stressed out.'

'I'm not sure about Imogen – all she wants to do is to marry Alex, and she can do that minus a cake and a few wedding favours. She's not in the least bit concerned about all the bells and whistles, but her mum Julia is obsessed with the details, right down to the release of a kaleidoscope of butterflies when they exchanged their vows.'

'So where are the wedding party today?'

'I'm not absolutely sure. I got a text from Imogen to say she couldn't make it, so Ella and I decided to whip up a few dozen of our amazing cupcakes instead; there's a batch for you to hand out your customers with their coffees and a batch to take up to the hotel to cheer Julia up.'

'Nothing like a sweet treat to bring a smile to your face! Thanks, Millie. You and Ella are really kind. I'm so lucky to have friends like you. I'm going to miss you when you leave. And, I'm sure I'm not the only one.' Lottie's eyes held a twinkle of mischief. 'How's Zach? We haven't seen him in the bar all week. Dylan was asking if you've got him locked away in that wooden lodge of his. Have you been keeping him busy with the cookery school stuff?'

'I… erm… no I haven't, actually.' Millie felt her stomach give an uncomfortable lurch as the disturbing image of Zach with his arms entwined round Chloe's slender waist floated across her vision. 'His girlfriend has arrived from the UK.'

'His girlfriend?' spluttered Lottie. 'Zach hasn't got a girlfriend. If you're talking about Chloe, they finished, like, months ago. He told Dylan all about their break-up before he came over to St Lucia – how she gave him an ultimatum about producing an engagement ring, so he decided it was the kindest thing to do to end the relationship before she got hurt even more. *And* hadn't she met a new guy? I heard that snippet of news straight from Zach's mouth and so did you! Didn't he propose to her at the top of the Eiffel Tower? I distinctly remember thinking how romantic that would be.'

'I know, I'm confused too. I don't know the details, I just know that Chloe is here and Zach's happy about it.'

Lottie's face screamed scepticism but she didn't have the chance to contradict Millie's interpretation because Millie's phone had sprung into life.

'Hi, Imogen.' Millie paused, resting her eyes on Ella's. 'No, it's no problem. Imogen, really, you don't have to apologise. Ella and I absolutely understand. In fact, we were on our way up to the hotel with a basket full of cupcakes to cheer everyone up. Great, then we'll see you in thirty minutes.'

Chapter Fifteen

'Wow, I thought Claudia's plantation house was picturesque, but this place is truly stunning,' said Millie, belatedly drawing her mouth closed as she surveyed the luxury boutique hotel nestled amid the manicured tropical gardens against the dramatic backdrop of the Pitons.

'Spectacular,' murmured Ella.

Millie stood on the pathway, lined with a welcome guard of honour fashioned from palm trees, and drank in the scene. A veil of tranquillity descended onto her shoulders and she felt all the stress of the day melt away from her temples. To her left was an area of decking laid out with wooden sun loungers and umbrellas overlooking the reason the hotel had been built there in the first place – probably the best view on the island of the Pitons. All around her, the soft melody of birdsong was accompanied by the rustle of leaves and the faint tinkle of running water. It was an oasis of calm in a chaotic world. She felt like she had fallen asleep and been transported to the Garden of Eden.

'Come on, we can't stay here. Imogen is expecting us,' whispered Millie, fearful of raising her voice and disturbing the peace.

Following the hand-carved signposts, Millie lead them along the meandering gravel pathways to the outside bar where Imogen had arranged for them to meet for a drink.

When they arrived, Millie almost laughed. With all its rustic charm, the bar at the Purple Parrot quite clearly occupied the opposite end of the spectrum from the drinking establishment that had emerged from within a canopy of glossy palm trees. With polished wooden floors and matching furniture, the place reeked of opulence and elegant splendour. The white muslin curtains, hung from the eaves to the floor, had been drawn back with twisted silk ties woven with gold threads. A large wooden trunk loitered in the corner with the word 'Games' stencilled along the side. Millie experienced a sudden urge to investigate but before she could do so, Imogen rushed into the bar.

'Millie! Ella! Oh, it's wonderful to see you.'

The bride-to-be exchanged kisses with them both. She looked stunning in an ivory linen sundress that just about skimmed her shapely thighs. Millie glanced down at her white capri pants and striped scarlet T-shirt and wondered why she hadn't been bestowed with a slice of the body-confidence pie. Then she reminded herself that Imogen had probably spent most of the last year preparing for the approaching weekend so it was no surprise she looked so polished.

'Thank you so much for coming. Are those the cupcakes you told me about on the phone? Oh, they look amazing! Gracie will love them.'

A white-jacketed waiter arrived with a silver tray holding a pitcher of mango juice and several crystal glasses. Millie thought of the psychedelic sludge Travis had served them earlier and smiled.

'Thanks, George. Do you think you could bring us a bottle of Laurent-Perrier, please?'

'Yes, madam.'

The last thing Millie needed was to indulge in more alcohol. She was still experiencing the after-effects of the white rum cocktail and if she added a glass or two of champagne to the mix she would be asleep all afternoon. While she didn't have anything other than a sun lounger calling her name, she wanted to make the most of every remaining moment at the villa and in the swimming pool before she boarded her flight back to the UK. Who knew when she would next see the sunshine?

'This hotel is absolutely gorgeous,' said Ella, sipping her mango juice, taking in her surroundings, clearly storing away every tiny detail so she could relate it all back to Denise later.

'It is,' smiled Imogen, staring at the view, the dark rings beneath her eyes apparent to even the most unobservant onlooker.

'Where are the men today?' asked Millie.

'Gone to watch a cricket match in the village. They should be back in an hour or so.'

The champagne arrived, along with Julia and Karen, and Millie had an idea.

'I'd love to see where your wedding ceremony is being held?'

'Oh, you'll love it. It's just the most romantic place to get married. Come on. Then, I'll show you the Hummingbird Suite where we're having our reception. Would you like to join us, Ella?'

'No thank you, dear. I think I'll just sit here with Julia and Karen and admire the view.'

The waiter popped the cork and poured three glasses of champagne, handing one crystal flute to each woman with a theatrical flourish.

'Perhaps you could bring another bottle, George,' said Julia, settling in for a gossip with Ella about the exhausting search she'd endured in the boutiques of London for mother-of-the-bride outfits suitable for a Caribbean wedding.

Imogen rolled her eyes at her mother and led Millie down the steps of the bar and onto the pristine lawns to the front of the hotel. Every single one of the borders was filled with a profusion of multi-coloured flowers, from scarlet to cerise, from vermillion to salmon-pink.

'The flowers are amazing,' said Millie.

'I agree. I spoke to one of the gardeners when we arrived and he told me that the hotel is blessed with fertile volcanic soil which means that even if you stick a wooden pole in the ground it will sprout leaves,' laughed Imogen. 'Here we are. What do you think?'

Looming in front of them like a wedding cake fashioned from white wrought iron and filigree, was the most perfect garden gazebo – an absolutely stunning location in which to exchange wedding vows. Millie expected to be transported back to her own debacle of an engagement party when her fiancé-to-be had failed to do her the courtesy of turning up, but she was surprised to find that the turmoil of emotions did not materialise. It was a revelation that made her smile.

'It is just the most amazing place. Sunday is going to be fabulous.'

'Thanks, Millie. I hope so. Mum's still anxious about the flowers not arriving in time. I think we'll be sorted in time for Sunday, but it definitely hasn't been the smooth, relaxed, tranquil experience she had been expecting. Nevertheless, one good thing has come out of it. Mum and Brad are like a pair of lovebirds and I'm so happy for her. It's about time she enjoyed a bit of romance.'

'St Lucia seems to have that effect on people,' thought Millie, not realising before it was too late that she had actually said the words out loud.

'What do you mean?' Imogen narrowed her eyes in curiosity.

'Oh, nothing. Weren't you going to show me the Hummingbird Suite?'

'Yes. Oh, you're going to love it, too! The walls have been hand-painted with beautiful humming-birds sitting in tropical foliage and the floral arrangements for the tables were supposed to be Birds-of-Paradise set in these amazing tall, slender glass vases. Mum hasn't been able to source them, so I'm not sure what we'll end up with.'

They had arrived in the corridor leading to the Hummingbird Suite. Despite the whole building having been taken over by Imogen and Alex's wedding guests, the hotel felt deserted. Apart from a lone gardener mowing the already pristine lawn next to the gazebo, Millie hadn't seen any other staff. Maybe the whole ethos of the place was that guests should feel as though they were visiting a friend's home rather than staying in a hotel – that's how she felt.

As they made their way towards the double doors, Millie's sandals clacked on the shiny wooden flooring like a pair of castanets. It was much cooler inside, with the air conditioning working overtime, causing goose pimples to ripple along her forearms.

'Okay. Ready to be amazed?'

'I am.'

Imogen grasped the brass handle and went to push the door open with a flourish, but it didn't budge.

'Oh, it's locked. That's strange. It wasn't locked when me and Mum came to check on the place settings earlier this morning.' Imogen gave the handle another wiggle for good measure and sighed.

'Don't worry. I'm sure it looks fantastic. I'll look forward to seeing the photographs on Facebook and Instagram,' laughed Millie.

'No. I'd really like your opinion on the layout of the top table. You've got a real sense of style, Millie, but I'm sure you're told that all the time.'

'Really?' Millie was about to utter a self-deprecating contradiction but stopped herself. It was about time she learned to have the confidence to accept compliments and to have more conviction in her own abilities.

'Come on. Let's find Jerome and ask him to open the doors.'

Imogen spun on her stilettos and marched off back down the corridor. They didn't have to search too hard to find the hotel manager, who was chatting to Greg and Carla on the pool terrace. Handsome enough to take the leading role in a Hollywood romcom, Jerome was clearly a man comfortable in his designer suit and starched collar despite the humidity. Millie caught a whiff of his expensive aftershave as he turned to welcome her to the hotel.

'Hi, Jerome. Can you unlock the Hummingbird Suite, please? I want to show Millie the table layout. I'm still not convinced about where the top table is.'

'Unlock it? But we never lock the doors to the Suite.' Jerome's dark brown eyes crinkled in confusion.

'Well, they are definitely locked now. We've just come from there.'

'No problem. I'm sorry you've been inconvenienced. I have the keys here.'

Jerome produced a bunch of silver keys from his pocket and strode towards the hotel with Imogen, Millie and Carla scampering in his wake. They reached the Hummingbird Suite and Jerome tried both the handles himself which caused Imogen and Millie to exchange a look of 'told you so'.

'Strange.'

Jerome selected a key, inserted it into the lock and pushed the door doors open. 'Voila!'

'Oh…'

'Oh my God!'

'Argh!'

Millie blinked, unable to believe what her eyes were telling her. Every table had been turned upside down, the linen tablecloths torn into pieces and scattered around the room like discarded wrapping paper, along with the serviettes. The silver cutlery had been strewn everywhere and the hummingbird paintings had been removed from the walls and stamped on. The room looked like a tornado had hit and done its worst.

'Oh, my God!' cried Imogen, her hand covering her mouth, tears collecting along her lashes. 'What…?'

Millie and Carla moved forward in unison to link Imogen's arms as Jerome dashed into the suite, rushing from table to table until he came to a sudden standstill, his gaze fixed on the wall to their right.

'Argh!' screamed Carla, who was the first to see what he was looking at.

When Millie followed Jerome and Carla's line of sight, her stomach dropped to her toes like an anvil down a well. Her heart flayed her ribcage so hard that she thought it would escape. Nausea threatened until she turned to see the expression on Imogen's face. If she and Carla hadn't been holding onto her she would have crumbled to the floor.

'What's…? Is that…?'

The maelstrom of destruction wasn't limited to smashed furniture and broken picture frames. Everything in the room had been doused in what Millie sincerely hoped was red paint; the floor boards, the drapes, the walls, even the crystal chandeliers. The whole place looked like a scene from the Caribbean Chainsaw Massacre.

'Is that blood?' muttered Carla, her eyes wide with horror.

Jerome was the first to pull himself together, yet his hands were shaking and his pallor had turned two shades lighter than it had been a few minutes earlier. He took a tentative step nearer the wall and sniffed.

'What are you doing?'

'It's not blood, Carla. This is tomato ketchup, and this,' he indicated the curtains and the floor, 'seems to be red spray paint.'

'But why would anyone…'

Imogen could hold onto her emotions no longer and burst into loud raking sobs, her body shaking uncontrollably.

'Someone doesn't want me and Alex to get married! They're doing everything in their power to destroy our wedding plans, but what I want to know is: why? What have we done to deserve this?'

'Carla, I think you should go and fetch Julia and Karen.'

'Right away.'

As Carla sprinted from the room, Millie lead the distraught Imogen to the only chair left standing and, with Jerome's assistance, settled her down in the seat and handed her a bunch of tissues from her pocket.

'I'm so sorry, Imogen. Please rest assured that the hotel will investigate this incident…'

'Darling!' cried Julia from the doorway, her hand flying to her chest as her eyes surveyed the damage. 'Oh my God! What in heaven's name happened in here? Is that blood?'

Before Julia and Karen had even taken a step into the room, a woman launched herself from behind an upturned table, a pair of kitchen scissors clutched in her fist raised high in the air, heading straight for Jerome.

Chapter Sixteen

'Oh my God! It sounds like the plot of a murder mystery show set on a Caribbean island,' declared Lottie, her eyes stretched wide with interest. 'So was Jerome hurt?'

Millie and Ella had returned to the Purple Parrot to give the wedding party some privacy whilst they came to terms with what had happened and decided what they wanted to do about their wedding arrangements. It was clear to everyone that the reception couldn't take place in the Hummingbird Suite.

'Superficial cuts to his arm and chest. He's been taken to hospital for stitches.'

'Poor Jerome. What on earth had he done to deserve that? Surely it couldn't have been a disgruntled guest!'

'Well, you're not going to believe this, but Jerome did know his attacker.'

'Who was it?'

'Fleur Markham.'

'Who's Fleur Markham?'

'She's Imogen and Alex's wedding planner.'

'Really?'

'Well, she only met with them once. Imogen and Alex did think it was strange that she had disappeared, but they never expected anything like this to happen.'

'And she decided to wreck the place and then stab Jerome with a pair of scissors, because…?'

'It turns out Imogen's mother, Julia, was right all along. Fleur and Jerome have history.'

'It's a very disturbing story,' muttered Ella, who had been uncharacteristically quiet since they had arrived at the bar, clearly very upset at the personal tragedy that had unravelled before their eyes. She twiddled the stem of the empty wine glass on the table in front of her, her eyes fixed on a spot on the horizon where the sea met the sky.

'What sort of history?' pressed Lottie, refilling everyone's glass with a tot of rum: her prescription for the recent shock.

'Apparently, a few months ago, Jerome ditched Fleur and ran off with her cousin. He had to leave his job as a hotel manager in Rodney Bay because Fleur was constantly harassing him after he'd terminated their relationship – he thinks she must have gone a little bit crazy. She had no idea he had relocated to Soufrière and found a new position at a local hotel; he thought he was safe. But as fate would have it, when she met with Imogen and Alex to discuss their wedding last Sunday, she caught a glimpse of Jerome in the hotel lounge. She returned later and sought him out — that was when Julia saw them arguing by the gazebo.'

'So what's happening about the wedding reception? I take it the Hummingbird Suite will be out of action for a good few weeks? Oh, no, don't tell me they have to call off the wedding? That would be just too awful!'

Millie saw Lottie cast a quick glance out into the bay where Dylan's boat was on its way back to shore after that morning's diving excursion. The expression of undiluted adoration on her pretty face made Millie think of Zach and her heart gave an uncomfortable kick. Because of everything that had happened over the last few hours, she hadn't had a chance to dwell on what he and Chloe were doing, but now she remembered that Chloe had said they would have a full itinerary. What if Zach had taken her to Treetop Adventures? She was more upset than she cared to admit about that possibility.

'Ella and I left before any decisions about the wedding were made, but Jerome couldn't be more apologetic. He honestly didn't connect the kitchen fire incident – the one that destroyed Imogen's wedding cake and favours earlier in the week – with Fleur. We know she was responsible for that too because when Alex and Greg arrived to drag her off Jerome she was screaming incoherently about the kitchen fire and how she had hoped he'd be caught up in it or sacked for the damage.'

'How utterly dreadful,' murmured Ella, her brown eyes filled with compassion for all the players in the story.

'So where is Fleur now?'

'She was also taken to the hospital with cuts to her hands. The paramedics sedated her and I think I heard them mention a referral to psychiatric services.'

Silence descended around the table as each of the women contemplated the recent turn of events.

'Hey! Why the long faces, girls? Aren't you sitting in the best bar in the Caribbean, ably managed by the most wonderful woman on the island of St Lucia?' Dylan leaned down to deposit a kiss on the top of Lottie's head, causing a splash of colour to appear on her pale cheeks and her eyes to dance with delight. 'Drinks are on me this afternoon. Just finished diving the coral reef with a bunch of corporate types from Texas who insisted on rewarding me with a huge tip!'

Dylan grinned as he shoved his palms deep into the pockets of his cut-off denim shorts and meandered towards the bar where he greeted Travis with a friendly handshake and slap on the back. Millie watched the two men share a joke, her heart ballooning at their display of relaxed camaraderie, and her faith in human nature leapt up a notch.

'So what do you think will happen about the wedding?' asked Lottie, her eyes still resting on her boyfriend, who wouldn't have looked out of place carrying a surf board along Waikiki Beach with his tanned features, sun-bleached hair and the leather thong around his neck sporting a huge shark's tooth.

'I really don't… Ah, well, perhaps you can ask Imogen that question yourself.'

Millie nodded in the direction of the wooden steps leading up to the veranda from the beach where Imogen was kissing Alex goodbye, before waving him off with Greg and Owen. Carla and Harriet followed their friend onto the terrace.

'Is it okay to join you?'

'Of course!' said Lottie, leaping from her chair. 'I'll get you some drinks – on the house.'

Imogen dropped into a padded cane chair next to Millie. Every ounce of her previous vitality seemed to have seeped from her body. Her eyes were still pink from the copious tears she had shed and her skin had taken on a translucent sheen. She let out a long, ragged sigh, and her resigned shoulders slumped into her chest.

'Alex thought it would be a good idea for us to get away from the hotel for a while. He's gone to the Blue Orchid with the guys, but I thought I'd find you both here. Karen and Gracie have gone on a shopping trip to Castries with a few of the other guests. Mum's distraught, understandably, but Brad has taken her to the Sulphur Springs for a detox to soothe her nerves and I'm sure he'll work his magic to calm her down.'

Imogen attempted a watery smile but she couldn't quite pull it off. She grabbed a beer mat from the table and started to pick at the edges. Millie's heart went out to her. None of what had happened had anything to do with Imogen or Alex, they were just innocent bystanders caught in the crossfire of a toxic relationship breakdown.

'I'm so sorry this happened, Imogen.' Millie reached over the table and squeezed Imogen's hand. 'What have you and Alex decided to do about the wedding?'

'Well, we could have had the reception out on the lawns at the front of the hotel. There's a spectacular view of the Pitons and plenty of space for the tables. However, when the staff were escorting Fleur from the premises, she not only confessed to the destruction of the furniture and decorations in the Hummingbird Suite, but she also hinted that she may have tampered with the food in the fridges.'

'What?'

'She refused to elaborate, and it's unlikely she was able to gain access to the kitchen this morning without any of the breakfast chefs seeing her, but we can't take the risk of poisoning our guests. So…' Imogen gulped down the gin cocktail Lottie had set in front of her and ran her tongue along her lower lip. 'Alex and I have decided to cancel the wedding. Alex is philosophical. He says it'll be a great dinner party story to share with our friends when we're old and grey.'

All six women fell into a contemplative silence as they sipped their drinks and entertained their own thoughts on the fiasco that had taken place in their midst. Millie's heart ached for Imogen and Alex, whose long-awaited wedding had been so effectively destroyed, and by their very own wedding planner to boot! You couldn't make it up. Then something occurred to her.

'Weren't you getting married in the gazebo in the hotel grounds?'

'Yes, it's a really beautiful spot.'

'And *it's* still there, isn't it? Fleur didn't set fire to *that*, did she?'

'No, the gazebo's still standing. Why?'

Millie's mind raced down an idea super-highway. Perhaps Imogen and Alex's wedding could be salvaged if everyone pooled their ideas and resources.

'So it's really just the wedding *reception* that's had to be cancelled?'

'Yes, I suppose so. But our guests have travelled thousands of miles to see us exchange our vows. We can't have a wedding without a wedding reception.'

'I might just have an idea.'

Chapter Seventeen

'What sort of thing do you have in mind?' Imogen's eyes brightened. She stopped fidgeting with the beer mat and pushed herself up in her chair, leaning towards Millie with her eyebrows raised.

Millie cast a quick glance across to Ella, who gave a gentle nod of agreement, followed by a beaming smile.

'Why don't you hold your wedding reception at the villa?'

'At the Paradise Cookery School?'

'Yes. I'm sure Claudia wouldn't mind. Thirty-six guests are a little more than she would probably envisage for a cookery course, but there's plenty of room for tables in the courtyard. We can use the kitchen to prepare the food – there're five ovens and plenty of workspace. If Jerome is prepared to release a couple of the hotel chefs to come over to the villa to help with the preparations and the cooking, I'm sure we can sort something out.'

'Wow! That's a fabulous idea!' exclaimed Harriet, clapping her hands in excitement.

'Have our wedding reception at the Paradise Cookery School,' murmured Imogen almost to herself as she took a few moments to allow the suggestion to sink in to her befuddled brain, a necklace of fresh tears appearing along her lower lashes. She glanced from Millie to Ella and back again, her expression morphing from dejection to excitement and newborn hope. 'Yes. Yes! I'd love that. Actually, it's perfect; the view is stunning and the photographs will be spectacular. Oh, are you sure you both want to do this?'

'Of course, it might not be the glamorous affair you and Alex had intended...'

'Mum intended...'

'But I think it'll be a wonderful day. Have your ceremony as arranged in the hotel gazebo and then bring your wedding party over here for the reception. You can use all the facilities – the pool, the veranda, the decking, the courtyard – and we'll sort out the food.'

'Oh, that sounds absolutely amazing! Thank you, oh, thank you.' Imogen shot out of her chair and hugged Millie, then Ella, and finally Lottie for good measure. 'I'll call the hotel and arrange for a couple of the chefs to help you, Millie. I don't think they'll mind – it's just a change of venue, after all. Oh, I've got to find Alex and tell him!'

Without pausing for breath, Imogen rushed off to tell her fiancé that they were getting married after all, albeit in a scaled-down version – just as they had both secretly wanted.

'Wait for me!' shouted Carla, launching herself from her seat, her trusty camera swinging around her neck. Out of respect, she had abstained from taking any photographs of the marriage meltdown as Imogen certainly didn't look her elegant best. But now she was on a mission to record the final chapters in the Caribbean fairy story. 'I want to grab a photograph of the look on Alex's face when you tell him! Come on, Harri. Last one to the Blue Orchid buys the champagne!'

The two bridesmaids clattered down the steps in Imogen's wake, giggling as they tried to run through the sand towards the main street without looking like a pair of clowns. Oh, how a few minutes could change a mood, thought Millie joining them in their happiness.

'Are you mad?' laughed Lottie when they were out of earshot. 'Do you know what you're letting yourself in for?'

Millie beamed at Lottie and Ella. The doldrums she had started the day fighting had disappeared off to plague some other underserving soul. She felt buoyant; a zoom of confidence had erupted in her chest and she was more excited about the future than she had been for months. Organising Imogen and Alex's wedding reception was exactly the type of challenge she loved getting stuck into and her fingers tingled with the urge to start on the preparations to make the celebrations the best she'd ever organised.

'When I worked at the restaurant in Oxford with Luke, we regularly did more than a hundred covers every night. I know I'm probably a bit rusty, but thirty-six wedding guests should be a doddle compared to that.'

Millie glanced around the Purple Parrot which was experiencing a lull in trade after the lunchtime customers had left for an afternoon's hiking in the Pitons, or to explore the tiny coves further along the coast, or to simply soak up the sunshine around their hotel pools.

'And I'm sure you do more than thirty-six meals here at the Purple Parrot every day?'

'Yes, but it's not gourmet-standard food,' smiled Lottie, flicking her hair over her shoulder. 'It's freshly prepared Caribbean fare with lots of local spices and chunky marinades and locally sourced meats and fish – barbequed. Simple, but delicious.'

'And that's exactly what I intend to offer Imogen and Alex's guests. There's no point in trying to replicate the menu on offer up at the luxury five-star hotel. So, I think we should give our guests a taste of the real Caribbean, showcase the vibrancy of the flavours and colours that St Lucia is famous for.'

'You keep saying we…'

'Ella and I, and anyone else I can press-gang into helping us out – even if it's just for a few hours to help get the courtyard set up with the tables and chairs. I think we'll be okay with the food side of things if Jerome agrees to loan us a couple of his chefs to assist in the kitchen, but we'll need a few waiters, and someone to be in charge of the bar, and of course, a Master of Ceremonies.'

'Well, you have the perfect candidate for that role already on site.'

'Who…? Oh, no, Lottie, I'm not asking…'

'You don't have any choice. Who else do you have on your list that is more qualified?'

'I was actually thinking of asking Henri.'

Millie shot a pleading glance across to Ella, hoping she would be able to persuade her son to don his best suit and direct the show with his habitual grace and aplomb.

'Henri would be delighted, dear,' smiled Ella. 'And I'm sure he'll be able to pitch in with arranging the tables tomorrow, but I happen to know that he has a trip to Martinique planned for Sunday to interview a local politician about the recent increase in the drug-running trade on the island for his newspaper. He's been researching the article for weeks. I think if he cancels his appointment, it will give the guy another excuse to delay and it'll be months before Henri gets another chance to grill him.'

Millie's mood deflated like a pricked balloon and it must have shown on her face because Lottie giggled. 'That's sorted then. Shall I ring Zach with the good news?'

'No need. I'll do it.'

'Great. Now that we've got that organised, I'll ask if Anisha will cover for me this weekend and you can count me in for tomorrow. Maybe Travis can have a word with Leon to put in a couple of hours too. I know Dylan will definitely help as soon as he finishes his last boat trip of the day. What are you waiting for? Hadn't you better start writing a shopping list?'

'I'll call Denise,' announced Ella, rushing off to use the Purple Parrot's telephone.

'Millie, whatever's going on with Zach and Chloe you need to talk to him about it. It's not good to let misunderstandings fester. I know all about that after what happened with me and Dylan. Honesty and openness is the best policy when it comes to lasting relationships.'

'We're not in a relationship…'

'Friendships are relationships. There is no reason why you and Zach can't still be friends, even if he is back with Chloe. I know you don't want to get hurt again after what happened with Luke, but in order for relationships to work we have to be prepared to let people into our hearts. It's the price we pay for a chance at happiness.'

'How did you get so wise all of a sudden?'

'Experience. Ring Zach, explain what's happened at the hotel, and ask him to be your Master of Ceremonies. He'll be amazing – and you know he'll make sure that everything runs like clockwork! Don't Imogen and Alex deserve that after what they have been through?'

'They do.'

'So, call him now before you overthink it. You don't have to talk about your feelings if you don't want to, but make friends. You can't go on avoiding each other. It'll just prolong the hurt.'

Millie didn't want to confess to Lottie that until the devastating news of Imogen and Alex's wedding cancellation, avoiding Zach was exactly what she had planned to do. Lie low, steer clear of the part of the cocoa plantation where his wooden lodge was situated, and then catch her flight back to London on Monday morning. She would never have to set eyes on Zach Barker ever again. She knew she would get over what had happened – she had a precedent with Luke to show her which path to follow. What would make it more difficult was that Zach had been instrumental in helping her to escape from dwelling on her past and showing her that concentrating on living in the present and looking forward to the future were the only way to achieve contentment. She had a lot to be grateful to him for.

'Okay, I'll call Zach.'

'Great.'

Lottie continued to stare at Millie as she drained her glass. 'What?'

'I'm not leaving until I see you dial his number.'

Millie rolled her eyes. 'Okay, okay. Look – I'm ringing him!'

She removed her phone from her pocket and selected Zach's number, her heart hammering a cacophony of trepidation as she anticipated hearing his voice for the first time since he had hared off to pick Chloe up from the airport.

'Hello?'

'Hi, Zach. It's me – Millie.'

Lottie pushed herself out of her seat, gave Millie a smile of approval, and made her way to the bar where Ella, Travis and Anisha were chatting about what they could do to help with the wedding arrangements.

'Hello, Millie, I was about to call you…'

'Great, so I'm not disturbing you. Look, something awful has happened and I need your help. Well, no, Imogen and Alex need your help.' And she went on to explain in as few words as possible about the nightmare their wedding had become.

'Gosh, so Maddening Millie stepped into the fray!' laughed Zach. 'Why am I not surprised to find you right in the middle of a maelstrom of misfortune? I dread to think what the villa's kitchen is going to look like after you've prepared a five-course meal for thirty-six wedding guests. Shall I book in a troop of industrial cleaners for Monday morning?'

'Actually, that might not be a bad idea,' Millie laughed as a warm feeling of gratitude for having reconnected with Zach invaded her body. 'But I was hoping you could do a bit more than make a few calls?'

'Of course. You know me; happy to help if I can.'

'How does the title of Master of Ceremonies sound? Or rather, a sort of Director of Operations who makes sure everyone is in the right place at the right time. There's no one better qualified to ensure that everything runs like clockwork – except maybe Carla's boyfriend Greg but he's a guest so I can't ask him.' Millie swallowed down the surge of emotions that had poked their head above the parapet when she said, 'You are an amazing organiser and I know Imogen and Alex would appreciate your assistance.'

'Would *you* appreciate my assistance?' asked Zach, a hint of mischief in his voice.

The thought of having to spend the next two days in close contact with Zach, with the spectre of a disapproving Chloe lurking in the background watching their every move, filled Millie with dread. However, she was willing to put her own feelings to one side and do whatever it took to pull off the audacious attempt to hold a wedding at the Paradise Cookery School. After all, this wasn't about her, and it wasn't about Zach and Chloe. It was about two people who had put aside their own desires for a quiet wedding to keep Imogen's bereaved mother happy. Imogen hadn't deserved what Fleur had done, but Millie knew she would take comfort from the fact that Fleur had acted out of the pain of unrequited love and her actions had not been directed at them.

'I'll take your awkward silence as a yes. So, you can count me in. I'll give Henri and Dylan a call and we'll sort out the logistics. Are you sure you can cater for the guests from the villa's kitchen?'

'Imogen has promised to speak to Jerome. I'm sure he'll agree to release two of his chefs to help out with the prep tomorrow and the cooking on the day of the wedding. The kitchen up at the hotel has to be deep-cleaned before they can use it again so they would just be sat on their bottoms twiddling their thumbs anyway. The fact that all the guests will be away from the hotel for the afternoon and evening on Sunday will give the hotel's management the chance to get in the commercial cleaners without causing too much disruption.'

'Right. Sounds like a plan. So, Millie, now that I've got you on the phone, I want to talk to you about Chloe.'

'Sorry, Zach, must dash. So much to do, so little time. We'll speak later.'

She terminated their conversation with a flick of her finger. She already felt like her brain was about to explode with everything that she needed to do before Sunday came around; there simply wasn't room for the added complication of how she felt about Zach.

Chapter Eighteen

'So, Travis has sorted out all the drinks and set up the bar on the terrace next to the pool,' said Ella, consulting the colour-coded list pinned to the clipboard she was holding. It was eight o'clock on Saturday morning and the villa was already abuzz with a frenzy of activity. 'And Henri and Leon have promised to rig up the microphone and music system in the courtyard when they get here this afternoon. Have you seen Zach?'

'Yes, he's helping Dylan arrange the tables with a couple of guys from the hotel. The whole place is already looking fabulous, don't you think?'

Millie indicated the garlands of bridal bunting Imogen's mother had just finished attaching to every tree bordering the courtyard. Julia had also brought Karen and Gracie's hand-made offerings – long strings of white ribbon, with butterfly shapes cut from plain white photocopier paper attached, fluttered in the morning breeze just like the real thing. She had announced that she loved them, preferred them in fact, and Millie had to agree with her.

Having completed the decorations to her exacting standards, Julia shot off to direct the tables-and-chairs operation, ensuring each was at precisely the right angle, insisting on several tweaks when the aesthetics didn't please her. Freshly laundered white linen cloths from the hotel were then draped over the tables and their addition transformed the courtyard into a fairy-tale wedding venue. Millie could imagine how romantic it would look when they switched on the fairy lights as darkness fell.

'She's an amazing woman, isn't she?' said Ella, as Julia delved into the boxes that contained the matching serviettes and began to fashion them into a very accomplished version of a swan. 'And how fortunate she is to have been given a second chance at love. It's the St Lucian rhythm of life weaving its romance through the hearts of its visitors. I know you've felt it too, Millie.'

Millie managed to stop herself from rolling her eyes at Ella. She had no intention of being drawn into a conversation that featured the words romance, love or relationships. Nevertheless, Ella's comment caused her to surreptitiously scour the throng for a glimpse of Zach.

There he was, right in the middle of things, directing the show with poise and efficiency, allowing Julia to take the lead role in the design of the backdrop for her daughter's wedding, but at the same time making sure the layout was practical and safe. The last thing they wanted was for someone to trip over a loose wire – or fall into a ditch.

As Millie had suspected, the set-up was progressing like a well-oiled machine. No random passer-by would have guessed it was the first wedding to be held at the Paradise Cookery School. The flowers had been delivered straight to the villa that morning and were being kept cool in one of the bedrooms with the air-con on full blast. They were expecting the crockery and glassware to arrive from the hotel at midday and now all Millie and Ella had to do was the food shopping.

They had spent their time on Friday afternoon planning every part of the meal in careful detail, from the hors d'oeuvres to the fish course, from the main meal to the desserts and the petit fours. Millie experienced the familiar wriggle of excitement that every professional chef feels before the preparation of a celebratory feast, and she knew that if she managed to pull it off Imogen and Alex's wedding would be one of the major achievements of her professional life.

Her thoughts briefly lingered on the telephone conversation she'd had with Claudia the previous afternoon.

'Hi, Claudia, it's Millie.'

'It's great to hear from you, Millie, and I have to say I'm more than a little envious that you're over there soaking up the Caribbean sunshine whilst the UK is submerged under a cloud of incessant gloom. I don't think it's stopped raining since you left.'

'How are you feeling?'

'My doctor informs me that my leg is mending nicely, and he has congratulated me on taking his advice to rest for once, but I would much rather be in my kitchen whipping up a soufflé. I'm bored, Millie!'

'Claudia, erm… I've got a favour to ask you.'

'Ask away, darling! I owe you several!'

Millie had already provided Claudia with regular email updates about the incident with Imogen's wedding cake, and the subsequent amendments to the Chocolate & Confetti itinerary, so she'd given Claudia a quick summary of the events of Friday morning, culminating in a request, more a plea really, for her permission to use the Paradise Cookery School as a wedding reception venue. As Millie had expected, Claudia had been delighted to come to Imogen's rescue and expressed her envy once again that she wouldn't be there to join in all the fun.

'Oh, the poor girl! Her mother must be frantic. I'm more than happy to put the villa at your disposal on one condition.'

'Of course, anything.'

'Please, please send me some photographs!'

'That shouldn't be a problem,' Millie laughed. 'Carla, one of Imogen's bridesmaids, is a professional photographer. I know she will take the most amazing pictures.'

'Oh, then maybe I could ask her if I can use a few of them on my website and Facebook page to advertise the villa when Tim and I eventually get around to offering overnight accommodation to the Paradise Cookery School guests next year?'

'I'm sure Carla would be delighted.'

Before their conversation ended, Claudia had expressed her heartfelt gratitude to Millie, and Ella, for representing the Claudia Croft Cookery School in such a positive way and for being instrumental in turning a tragedy into a success. She promised to sing Millie's praises to Étienne but did add a stern but well-meaning postscript that she wanted to see Millie make more of her talents now that she had shown what she was capable of.

Finally, to Millie's delight, Claudia had gone on to suggest that she ask her boss for a week's extended leave in the run-up to Christmas so she could join her in the Cotswolds to present a segment on the Festive Feast cookery course in the first week of December. Millie had thanked her profusely and promised to talk to Étienne. When she had said goodbye to Claudia, Millie didn't think her euphoria could climb any higher.

So, the only blot on her happiness landscape that hectic Saturday morning was the current awkwardness between her and Zach. She had met with him the previous evening to thrash out the wedding arrangements but had orchestrated things so that both Ella and Henri had been present at all times to ensure there was no possibility of their conversation morphing into anything more personal than what colour the napkins were going to be.

To Millie's surprise, there had been no sign of Chloe, either on the veranda last night during their briefing, nor was she there helping them set up that morning. Perhaps Chloe had seen their discussions as work-related, and it was still early so she was probably catching up on her beauty sleep. Millie certainly had no intention of asking Zach about the reasons for his girlfriend's absence. She wasn't sure whether she was relieved that Chloe had stayed away or disgruntled that she hadn't turned up to offer her help when it was all-hands-on-deck. After all, the more the merrier when she looked down at the list of things that they still needed to do.

'Where's Clavie got to?' groaned Ella, slotting her arms through the handles of her canvas bag and stamping her feet in frustration at the taxi driver's shoddy timekeeping. 'Denise is supposed to be meeting us at Castries market in thirty minutes – we're going to be late!'

'Don't worry, Mum. I'll take you,' offered Henri, dangling his car keys from his index finger and ushering Ella and Millie towards his ancient little Fiat.

'Thank you, Henri,' smiled Millie.

The journey to Castries was uneventful. Millie took the opportunity to enjoy what would be her last glimpse of St Lucia's spectacular western coastline, and the picturesque villages that scattered the hillside, before she left for the airport on Monday morning. She truly hoped that she would have the opportunity to return to the island that had made such an impression on her heart, maybe for a holiday, or perhaps to co-present another course for the Paradise Cookery School. Despite the numerous hiccups, it had been the most amazing experience, the best three weeks of her life, in fact.

She was proud of what she had achieved, not only in the kitchen but on a personal level. She had emerged from beneath a veil of despondency that had seemed to stalk her every move since the break-up with Luke. She had been reminded that not only was she an accomplished chef, but that she could also help and encourage others to discover their own affinity with food of all varieties – not just chocolate-inspired. She knew she was back to her Cordon Bleu-trained best and the increase in her confidence felt amazing.

As Henri's little red Fiat navigated the numerous potholes, Millie continued to meander the corridors of her mind, counting her blessings and the reasons for them: Ella, Denise, Lottie, Henri, Dylan, but the person she had most to thank was there at centre stage. Zach, the most irritating, spiky, generous, handsome man she had ever had the good fortune to meet and, given a different set of circumstances, she knew she could easily have fallen in love with him.

Maybe she already had? Wasn't that the reason she couldn't stop thinking about the way his eyelashes fluttered against his cheeks when he closed his eyes, or how he had dragged her into his arms on the wooden platform high in the trees during their zip lining expedition? She couldn't deny her body's reaction when they had shared a goodnight kiss after a meal at his lodge before Imogen and her friends had arrived.

But was it simply physical desire? She doubted it. Whenever she was at Zach's side she experienced an avalanche of emotions that she'd never encountered during the time she had spent with Luke. Every single sense sparkled with excitement, her heart filled with a surfeit of happiness, and her lips tinkled with the desperate hope that he would kiss her. Those weren't feelings of mere sexual attraction and she wondered how their adventure would have ended if Chloe hadn't called when she did.

'Earth to Millie? Are you receiving?' laughed Henri as he skirted around a coach filling up with recently disembarked cruise passengers to snatch a parking space a few yards away from the capital's vibrant market. 'Look, there's Aunt Dennie!'

Sporting her usual attire of brightly coloured kaftan – today's a medley of orange, yellow and scarlet – and matching bandana, Denise waved at them, hoisting her over-large straw bag onto her shoulder and trotting on her kitten heels to meet them, a wide smile lighting up her handsome features.

'Thanks, Henri. See you back here in an hour?' said Millie.

'No problem. Make sure you get everything you need, though. We won't have time to make a return trip.'

'Okay.' She gave Henri a quick peck on the cheek and climbed out of the rust bucket formerly known as a Fiat 500. 'Hi, Denise. Thanks ever so much for coming.'

In response, Ella's best friend collected Millie into her arms and gave her an affectionate squeeze. A tantalising whiff of gardenias floated to Millie's nostrils causing her to smile and her gratitude to burgeon further.

'Millie, my darling, what's this I hear about you offering to put on a wedding feast with only twenty-four hours' notice? Are you crazy, girl? Do you have sunstroke, or perhaps you've been partaking in a little too much of the local rum? Or could it be something else that's causing you to lose your senses?' A twinkle of mischief appeared in Denise's eyes.

'Millie isn't crazy, Dennie,' said Ella as she led them into Castries market to do battle with the stall holders. 'She has a heart of gold. Now, were you able to source absolutely everything on the list I gave you over the phone last night?'

Millie and Ella had collaborated with Imogen and Alex to decide on the new menu that would, as far as possible, incorporate their favourite dishes and flavours. After champagne and canapés on arrival, the wedding guests would be seated at their tables in the courtyard and served a starter of carrot and sweet potato soup, followed by poached red snapper marinated in a lime-and-chilli dressing – both Alex's choice. Apparently, his gran had made the best carrot and coriander soup in the whole of Lancashire.

Imogen had chosen the main course and they would be preparing jerk chicken breast with sides of butternut squash mashed with mango, brown sugar and a squeeze of lime and either a medley of fresh Caribbean vegetables – peas, okra and a hint of mint – or an apple, pomegranate seed and coriander salad. Of course, the dessert had to be chocolate-inspired and Imogen had requested a dark chocolate torte with Caribbean rum-infused ice cream. There would also be a huge bowl of tropical fruit salad – guava, kiwi, passion fruit, pineapple.

'You know me, Ella,' chuckled Denise. 'I've been here since seven a.m. tracking down the freshest produce St Lucia has to offer! All the fruit, vegetables and salad items have been packed into crates and Marlin has agreed to deliver everything to the villa this afternoon along with the chicken breasts and the red snapper. The home-made bread and cheeses are ready for us to collect, but I thought you and Millie would like to select your own herbs and spices so you get the best that's on offer today. I just know that Imogen and Alex are going to have the most wonderful Caribbean wedding breakfast. Come on, let's get shopping!'

A surprise coil of anxiety snaked into Millie's chest. Denise had such confidence in her abilities, which was flattering but nerve-racking at the same time. She really didn't want anything to go wrong, not because it would reflect on her culinary competency, but because of the effect any inadvertent 'Millie Mishaps' would have on Ella and Claudia. She took a deep breath and lifted her chin – she was determined not to let that happen.

'Wow! I love these anthuriums. They're a lovely heart-shape and a perfect red colour – ideal for a wedding! Why don't we buy a few to display around the pool?' said Ella.

Millie glanced at the plants Ella was fingering. To her, the flowers had always looked a bit indecent with the protruding fleshy spike and she wasn't sure they would be the best choice for a wedding – or maybe they were. She felt her lips twitch as she met

Denise's eyes and couldn't prevent a giggle from erupting. Denise joined her with a deep raucous belly laugh.

'Oh, my God! Get a grip you two!' chastised Ella, shaking her head at their playground antics.

'Perhaps we should go with these Barbados lilies instead?' compromised Millie. 'The pink ones are gorgeous and they smell amazing – and look, they're called True Romance. It's a sign!'

Ella had already moved on to the next table, nodding a friendly greeting to the stallholder.

'I think this lemon mint will make a delicious addition to a lemon and lime sorbet, just in case anyone doesn't fancy the dark chocolate torte or fruit salad.'

Despite the early hour, the market was bustling with people – locals and tourists alike. The aromas were intoxicating and Millie raised her nose to inhale the sharp exotic fragrances, closing her eyes to savour the sensation and to store the memory away in the crevices of her mind so she could take it out and relive the experience when she got back home.

From that morning onwards, the smell of nutmeg would forever be associated with her stay on St Lucia. Every time she grated it into one of her patisserie recipes, she would be transported back to the sun-filled days she had spent at the Paradise Cookery School and at the Botanical Gardens where she had seen it growing in its indigenous environment. Of course, those memories would be inextricably linked with Zach, because he had been by her side on that day trip, but she was okay about that. His presence at Claudia's villa had enhanced her all-too-brief sojourn in the tropical paradise and she was grateful for his friendship even if it *had* ended so abruptly with the arrival of Chloe.

'Okay, have we got everything we need?' asked Denise, her plump arms laden with brown paper carrier bags crammed to bursting with fresh produce.

'Is that a coconut? Since when did we have coconuts on our shopping list?' laughed Ella, teasing her oldest friend.

'I couldn't resist it. Hey, Angus, would you give us a hand to carry our purchases to the car, please?' Denise called to one of the store holders who was relaxing behind his display of intricately carved masks, his feet resting on a wooden crate, a cigarette protruding from his lips. He didn't look overjoyed to be asked to leave the comfort of his deckchair.

After a brief struggle to squeeze shut the boot of Henri's Fiat, Millie, Ella and Denise jumped in for the return journey to Soufrière. The temperature had climbed steadily whilst they had been saun-tering around the market stalls and the little car was like an oven.

'It'll be okay once we get out of Castries and onto the open road,' promised Henri. 'Did you get everything on your lists?'

'We did. Now all we have to do is peel, slice, chop, whip and cook up a storm!' Ella erupted into one of her signature belly laughs. 'My favourite pastime.'

'Mine too,' added Millie.

'Well, I do love the cooking,' smiled Denise, her brown eyes sparkling with pleasure at being a part of the culinary gang that day. 'But the tasting part has to be in the top spot of the hit parade for me.'

'Are you looking forward to your trip to Martinique tomorrow, Henri?' asked Millie, keen to divert attention from the wedding for a few moments.

'I am. I've waited months to speak to Jacques Barnier about what the authorities are doing to prevent young people from becoming involved in the drugs trade. I'm planning a full feature article for *The Soufrière Tribune*, but I'm also going to send the piece to a contact of mine on *Le Monde* which will hopefully mean that whatever promises

Monsieur Barnier makes can't be simply brushed under the carpet once we've published.'

'I hope you get what you need, Henri. I'd like to read your article when it's finished.'

'Thanks, Millie.'

Millie saw from Henri's tightened jawline how much the subject matter of his interview meant to him and whilst she would have loved his calm, level-headed presence at Imogen and Alex's wedding, she knew what he was doing was much more important in the wider scheme of things.

Chapter Nineteen

Ten minutes later, they arrived at the villa and Millie's heart ballooned with joy at the sight that met her eyes. The whole place looked magical, like a wedding-themed grotto set amongst the palms tress and lush tropical vegetation. If she was ever lucky enough to have a wedding day, she wanted exactly the same kind of backdrop for exchanging her vows. She smiled to herself, recognising that even the aspiration was a huge step forward in her recovery process from the heartbreak Luke had caused. Only a few weeks ago she would never have been able to contemplate a future wedding day, let alone one that caused her to smile so widely.

'Doesn't it all look fantastic!' exclaimed Ella, clapping her hands with excitement. She leapt from the back seat of the Fiat and, along with Denise, shot across to greet Zach and Dylan with exuberant hugs, chattering about the produce they had purchased at the market.

Millie followed more slowly in their wake, her stomach churning with a kaleidoscope of errant butterflies when Zach's gaze met hers over the shoulder of an extraordinarily handsome man who was holding a coil of black cable as though it were a venomous snake.

'Hi, Millie, allow me to introduce Brad Maxwell, an old friend of Julia's who's very kindly agreed to help with the sound equipment. Brad, this is Millie Harper, culinary maestro at the Paradise Cookery School. You should taste her chocolate-and-chilli soufflés – they are delicious! Sadly, she refuses to share the recipe with anyone!'

'Great to meet you, Brad,' said Millie offering him her palm, but instead getting pulled into a tight embrace. Imogen had been right – at close quarters Brad *did* look like George Clooney's older brother. She was surprised to feel her cheeks flush with heat so she turned her back on the four men to survey the courtyard. 'It's all absolutely gorgeous! What do Imogen and Alex think?'

'Actually, Julia thought it would be better to keep it as a surprise,' explained Brad, his voice deep and gravelly with the hint of an American accent. 'They've been dispatched to the Diamond Falls for the afternoon with Carla and Greg, and Harriet and Owen. But you're right, the whole place looks as though it was made for wedding ceremonies – intimate, relaxed, romantic.'

When Brad smiled his eyes crinkled attractively at the corners and Millie understood why Julia had spent so much time in his company over the last week. Not only that but he smelled like a Parisian perfumery, and he endeared himself to her even more when he asked, 'Need any help in the kitchen? We're just about finished out here.'

'Oh, that's really kind of you, but I think we've got everything under control – or we will have once the hotel chefs arrive. Is there any sign of them yet?'

'Yes, they arrived half an hour ago. They've made a start setting up the catering equipment they brought with them.'

'Although I'm sure Millie will probably need to take you up on your offer tomorrow morning, Brad. You should see the state of the villa's kitchen after a day with Messy Millie at the helm,' interjected Zach, giving her a mischievous wink.

Millie considered issuing a witty retort but chose to ignore his comment. However, what she couldn't ignore was the effect his proximity was having on her. She experienced an overwhelming urge to reach out and touch his muscular forearms, to trail her fingertips along the scattering of hairs that had been bleached gold by the Caribbean sunshine. She felt as if her breath had been trapped in her chest and that her light-headedness was due to the lack of oxygen, but of course it wasn't. The man standing before her, eyes dancing with amusement, had flicked a switch in a part of her body she had scarcely known existed. And if she had thought Brad's cologne was potent, it was nothing compared to the divine fragrance emanating from Zach and she almost swooned.

He had seen her reaction and his lips curved into a smirk, producing those cute dimples that caused her heart to flutter uncontrollably. Damn him! Why did she have to discover there was an undeniable chemistry between them when his girlfriend was back on the scene? She was so the mistress of bad timing!

She spun on her heels and followed Ella and Denise to the veranda where a tray of drinks had been left for the workers to help themselves. She poured herself a glass of home-made lemonade and she had never tasted such sweet nectar. As the ice-cold liquid slipped easily down her throat, a sudden image of Zach swimming in the pool floated across her vision – minus swimming trunks!

Oh, for goodness' sake, Amelia Harper! Get a grip, she chastised herself.

She knew that the sooner she submerged herself into the cooking the better, otherwise she would end up a melted mass of hormones. She paused on the threshold to the kitchen where two young men in chef whites were busily helping Ella and Denise to unpack their shopping baskets, chatting about the menu, making suggestions for variations, and generally indulging in what a chef liked best – talking about food.

'Ah, Millie, there you are,' said Ella. 'Boys, this is Amelia Harper, but it's Millie to friends. Millie, this is Marcel and Eddie. Eddie went to school with Henri and I've known him since he was six years old. I am now entirely confident that this wedding reception will be perfect. Eddie is a genius with fish dishes. His grilled lobster with coconut and lime marinade is to die for.'

Millie bumped fists with Eddie and then Marcel before grabbing an apron and a kitchen knife. To the strains of a jaunty reggae rhythm, the fivesome spent the rest of the afternoon and early evening slicing, chopping, squeezing, whisking, gutting and sculpting, until everything that could be prepared in advance had been stored in the huge Smeg refrigerator where there wasn't an inch of shelf space to spare.

Everyone worked together like a synchronised dance routine, no one claiming head chef status, no one relegated to washer-upper. The jerk chicken was marinating, the carrot and sweet potato soup had been made, and Ella had created a mouth-watering lemon-and-lime sorbet with a hint of fresh mint from the garden. All the vegetables were prepared and Denise had been given a lesson by Marcel in vegetable sculptures and had produced a passable rose from a cucumber.

Millie had been responsible for baking the dark chocolate tortes. She had made many variations on the chocolate torte theme during her career in the kitchen, but she had decided to use a recipe from one of Claudia's cookery books. She knew Claudia would be delighted and she was proud of how they had turned out.

By the time Marcel and Eddie had finished wiping down the benches, twilight had begun to tickle the horizon sending long shards of apricot and salmon pink into the sky. Storm lanterns and garlands of white fairy lights transformed the poolside terrace into a mesmerising place to rest weary bones and gulp down a celebratory glass of pomegranate juice before Marcel and Eddie headed home. Only Denise partook in a tot of rum to soothe away the tiredness, the others abstaining for fear of not being at their best the next day which they agreed would start at six a.m.

'See you tomorrow,' called Eddie as he and Marcel sped down the driveway on their motorbikes, revving their engines like boy racers. Ten minutes later, Henri appeared, poured himself a drink and crashed into one of the deckchairs next to Millie, expelling a long, ragged sigh.

'My God! Julia certainly knows how to squeeze the last ounce of strength from her band of volunteers. However, I'm here to report that everything now matches her vision for her daughter's nuptials. She and Brad said to tell you how grateful they are and that they'll see you tomorrow at the ceremony.'

'What? No, Henri, you must have misheard. I'm not invited to the ceremony at the hotel.'

'Well, you are now. Here.'

Henri handed her a thick white envelope with her name scrawled across the front in Julia's elegant handwriting. She ran her fingernail under the flap and withdrew the enclosed card, its edge embossed with gold, inviting her to attend the wedding ceremony of Miss Imogen Andrea Faversham and Mr Alexander Fredrick Watson.

'Mum was invited too, but she politely refused because she wants to oversee the final food preparations with Denise, Eddie and Marcel. Like everyone else, she loves a good wedding but she loves cooking more and this is her dream come true. And before you do likewise, I'll warn you in advance that resistance will be futile. Mum assured Julia that you will be there to see Imogen and Alex exchange their vows in the garden gazebo. I recommend you simply accept with good grace and enjoy the whole confetti-filled carnival.'

Millie held Henri's eyes for a moment, but the decision was surprisingly easy. Most of the preparation had been done, and even if she attended the wedding, she would still be able to get back to the villa in time to put the finishing touches to the canapés. Excitement whooshed around her body. Wow! She was going to be a guest at a luxury wedding in the tropical Caribbean paradise – what an amazing honour! She couldn't wait to call Jen to tell her. Then something else occurred to her. Had Julia invited anyone else?

'Has everyone gone home?' she asked, feigning nonchalance.

'Yes. Dylan's taken Zach for a drink at the Purple Parrot. I could give you a lift down to Soufrière before I drop Mum and Denise off, if you fancy joining them?'

'Oh, erm, no thanks,' she muttered, unsurprised at the dart of disappointment that shot through her chest. 'I think I should conserve my energy for tomorrow. We got lots done today, but tomorrow is going to be manic.'

Millie wondered why Henri hadn't mentioned that Chloe was with Dylan and Zach, but she didn't want to start that line of questioning. Despite having spent most of the afternoon in the kitchen, she had popped out to the courtyard to take a plate of sandwiches to the workers and there had still been no sign of Zach's girlfriend, which she thought was strange. Surely she had wanted to be with him at some point during the day, even if she did classify the wedding preparations as Zach's work?

'I don't mind admitting that I'm completely bushed,' complained Henri, stretching out his long legs and running his palm over the shadow of stubble that had appeared on his jawline. His mahogany eyes, identical in colour to his mother's, were ringed with tiredness and Millie smiled at her friend, who, like her, had French genes running through his blood. Whilst her Gallic roots were courtesy of her mother, Monique, who had met her father whilst he was on a backpacking holiday in Provence, Henri's had been inherited from a father he had not met until he was at university in France.

Ella had met Pierre, a student from Bordeaux, while he was holidaying on the island, but unlike Monique, her story did not have a happy ending. When Ella had told Pierre she was pregnant, he had caught the next flight back home to France and Ella had no choice but to raise Henri herself; not alone, but with the help and support of her family and friends. She had nurtured an intelligent, community-minded human being who campaigned fearlessly, via journalistic tenacious-ness, for improvements in the funding available for local projects to combat youth unemployment.

Millie tried to offer Henri a smile but was suddenly overtaken by a huge yawn as Ella and Denise appeared on the terrace from their final tour of inspection of the villa and the courtyard.

'Okay, Henri, I think we should leave Millie to get an early night. Tomorrow is going to be a very busy day. I hope you've agreed to attend the wedding ceremony, Millie?'

'I wouldn't miss it for anything!' she smiled, gratified to see the approval in Ella's eyes.

'Delighted to hear it. Good night, dear. Straight to bed, unless something better comes along!'

Ella guffawed at the look of astonishment her off-the-cuff comment had caused. She gathered Millie into a bear hug, the perfume of sweet jasmine floating in the air between them as Millie hugged her back. Denise did likewise, and then the two best friends ambled in Henri's wake to where he had left the Fiat, gossiping about another wedding they had attended when the groom had fallen into the hotel's pool.

Millie waved at the little car until its red tail lights disappeared from view. She locked the French doors and made her way through the court-yard to her studio above the garage, pausing at the front door to drink in the view. She wanted to fix the scene in her mind's eye as the epitome of paradise with the clicking of the cicadas, the chattering of the invisible night-time creatures, and the gentle swish of the palm fronds in the evening breeze.

She may be exhausted, but she had never been happier and she wished she could stop the world from turning so she could remain on that spot for ever. However, the cool, crisp sheets on her bed were calling her name and she was desperate to lay her head on the pillow and surrender herself to a deep and dreamless sleep.

Chapter Twenty

'Millie? Millie? Are you awake?'

She prised her eyes open and immediately screwed them shut again as the bright light sliced into her brain with surprising vigour.

'Millie?'

She pushed herself upright, made her way out to the balcony, and looked over the railings into the courtyard below. A sigh of satisfaction, mingled with relief, escaped from her lips. She hadn't dreamed it after all. The villa's courtyard really did look idyllic, and to add to the perfection of the image, standing in between the tables was Lottie, waving a paper bag in the air.

'At last, Sleeping Beauty emerges from her royal chamber,' her friend giggled. 'I've brought croissants. It's going to be a long day and I thought you might need something to kickstart your engines. Henri tells me you've been invited to the ceremony! So, are you going to come down and let me in or should I devour these buttery marvels on the doorstep?'

Millie's heart ballooned with gratitude at the friendship she had encountered since she arrived in St Lucia. Ella, Denise, Lottie, Anisha; they had all rallied round to offer their support when life conspired to toss random grenades in the path of orderliness and best-laid plans. With friends like them around, she knew she could face any challenge. She rushed down the stairs to let Lottie in, only belatedly realising that all she had on was a pair of cotton shorts and a camisole.

'Hi, Lottie, come on in, I'll put the kettle on and then you can help me decide what to wear.'

'Ah, now that's where having a friend who's a fashion connoisseur comes in handy.'

'What do you mean?'

Millie followed Lottie up the stairs, filled the kettle, and spooned instant coffee into two mugs as she had no energy to make a cafetière. She tore open the bag containing the croissants sending flakes of pastry cascading onto the counter top. The aroma of sweet, warm pastry was too much to resist and she crammed one the mini pains au chocolat into her mouth and rolled her eyes in ecstasy.

'Anisha has sent you this. I don't mind admitting that I'm soooo jealous that I won't be sitting next to you when Imogen and Alex tie the knot, just so I can see you in this creation of sartorial wonder. Go on, open it.'

Lottie removed a suit carrier from her shoulder and handed it over to Millie.

'But, how…'

'Henri popped into the Parrot last night and told us that Julia had invited you to the ceremony in the gazebo at the hotel. Anisha and I knew you would be panicking about what to wear so she rushed home to collect the dress she wore for her sister's wedding in the summer. It's absolutely stunning!'

Lottie's eyes sparkled with excitement as she took a seat in one of the cane chairs on Millie's tiny balcony, tossing her magenta hair over her shoulder as she sipped her coffee and settled down in her front row seat waiting for the impending fashion show.

Millie unzipped the bag and removed the most exquisite dress she had laid eyes on. Pale aquamarine in colour with a smattering of matching sequins outlining the neckline, it shimmered in the early morning sunlight like a waterfall.

'Try it on!'

'I don't know what to say…'

An avalanche of emotions ambushed Millie and a lump appeared in her throat. She couldn't believe

Anisha had offered to lend her such a beautiful garment. Tears gathered along her lashes and she tried to swallow down her feelings, but Lottie wasn't fooled and she ditched her coffee to draw Millie into a hug.

'You absolutely deserve to wear a dress like that to watch Imogen and Alex get married, Millie. If it wasn't for you, and Ella, the wedding would probably not be taking place. So, put the dress on, brush a little coconut oil through those gorgeous curls of yours and I'll give you a lift up to the hotel.'

'Thank you, Lottie. For everything. I couldn't have done any of this, the cookery school, the recipes, the wedding, without you and Ella and Denise, not to mention Dylan, Henri, Travis and Leon. You've all be so kind, and I feel like I've known you forever!'

'Haven't you missed someone from that list of amazing people?'

Millie experienced a squirm of discomfort. She had intended to keep her feelings for Zach locked securely away, with the key hidden in her pocket so that she could enjoy the celebrations without constantly wondering where he was and what he was doing, and more importantly who with.

'Look, Millie, I don't know what's going on with Zach and Chloe but trust your Auntie

Charlotte – they are not back together, I just know it. You absolutely have to talk to him before you leave tomorrow. I haven't said this to you, but there's something special between the two of you, something I can't quite put my finger on, but when you're together I can see the spark that you bring out in each other. Okay, lecture over. Now, off you go and get ready. You don't want to be late, do you? That the bride's prerogative.'

Millie decided that arguing with Lottie would only reaffirm what she knew already – her friend was right, she couldn't deny the feeling of elation whenever she was around Zach.

She took a quick shower then slid the dress over her body, buoyed up by the fact that it fitted like a second skin. She dragged a comb through her hair and managed to tame it into a passable chignon, trying not to remember the last time she had worn her hair like that. With a slick of nude lipstick and a spritz of the designer perfume Jen had given her for her birthday, she was ready to attend the first wedding since her broken engagement to Luke.

And yet, it wasn't Luke's face that was meandering through her thoughts. She could honestly say, hand on heart, that she felt no lingering regrets that their relationship had ended.

'Wow! You look fabulous, Miss Harper!' declared Lottie, hugging Millie for the third time in the space of thirty minutes causing her to cling tight onto her emotions with the last of her finger-nails. It wouldn't do to turn up at the wedding of the decade with bulging red eyes and tears on her cheeks.

Lottie drove Dylan's Jeep in the same carefree way she lived her life and by the time they swung into the hotel's car park, Millie felt as though she'd been dragged through the tropical rainforest on the back of a tractor. She patted down her hair, collected her purse and promised Lottie that she would hop into a taxi for the ride back to the villa as soon as the ceremony was over so that she could be back to help hand round the drinks.

She glanced around the pristine gardens at the front of the hotel. The neatly clipped lawns and flowerbeds were sporting a profusion of colourful flowers that could rival any English stately home, but what tipped the balance of magnificence was the view. The cerulean of the sky, the sapphire of the Caribbean Sea, the terracotta of the town's roofs at the foothill of the Pitons, the lush emerald landscape of their flanks, all melded together into a poem for the eyes.

She made her way to the hotel reception, surprised to find it was deserted; no sign of the nightmare that had taken place at the hotel over the last two weeks. She checked her watch – fifteen minutes to go – and made her way towards the rear of the hotel where the gazebo was situated, realising when she got there she was the last guest to arrive and every one of the pretty white seats, tied with pale pink ribbons, had been taken.

Several guests lingered at the back of the seating area, chatting to friends, laughing at jokes, exclaiming at the beauty of the scene. The wedding gazebo looked amazing, its white wrought iron-work entwined with a profusion of flowers, paper birds and butterflies. The hotel had clearly pulled out all the stops to make the venue as spectacular as possible.

Before Millie had a chance to enquire about extra seating, the string quartet struck up 'Ode to Joy' and she turned to see Imogen appear on the hotel terrace, walking proudly on her mother's arm along the red carpet, a wide beam of happiness on her face as she made her way towards where Alex was waiting for her in the gazebo. Millie couldn't control the turmoil of emotions as she watched Imogen stride towards her new life as Alex's wife, especially when she saw the bittersweet expression on Julia's face as she performed the role her late husband would have given anything to perform.

From her place at the back of the congregation, part hidden by the flower-decked white wooden screens that framed the wedding party, Millie listened to Imogen and Alex exchange their vows and then read a poem to each other they had written only the night before. It was a truly moving experience and there wasn't a dry eye in the garden afterwards, every single guest rising to their feet to applaud the newly-weds when they sauntered back down the aisle to accept the congratulations of their guests.

Imogen's dress was simple yet glamorous; a long strapless column of ivory silk with hundreds of crystals scattered from the waist to the hem glistening in the midday sun. She wore a single white orchid in her hair and carried a bouquet of white calla lilies and roses. Carla and Harriet looked amazing in matching ivory bridesmaid dresses, carrying posies of white and pink flowers to add a splash of colour to the ceremony, along with Julia's elegant pale pink mother-of-the-bride outfit that at one stage she had no doubt feared she would never get to wear.

The wedding guests obviously knew what had happened to Imogen's wedding cake and the favours, had gossiped *ad infinitum* about the devastation wreaked on the Hummingbird Suite by their wedding planner, and the reasons behind it. It was like a plot from a romcom movie, especially when it had looked as if the whole ceremony would have to be cancelled. The fact that it had been pulled off with such style was testament to what the power of love could achieve.

After offering her own congratulations, Millie decided to take a shortcut through the gardens back to the front driveway so she could get a head start on the guests heading for the wedding reception at the villa. Forgetting she was wearing unfamiliar heels, she lost her footing and stumbled into a huge camellia bush. Before she had chance to realise what was happening a pair of strong hands reached forwards and dragged her upright.

'Need a bit of assistance?' asked a familiar voice.

'I… what are you doing here?'

'Always the tone of surprise! Should I have left you in the bush?'

'No…'

The corners of Millie's mouth twitched, and when she met those dark brown eyes that had frequented her dreams more often than she cared to admit, her heart gave a sharp nip of desire and a giggle spluttered from her lips. She did make a habit of being rescued from arboreal catastrophes.

'Just so we're straight. I'm not a gatecrasher. Imogen and Alex invited me to the ceremony last night, but when I called round to collect you this morning, you had already left.'

Zach was standing inches away from her, his proximity causing those sparkles of electricity Lottie had referred to earlier. The heady fragrance of his lemony aftershave, mingled with the aroma from the flowers, caused her to close her eyes for a second to appreciate the olfactory sensation. When she opened them again, Zach's gaze scorched right through her.

'Millie, I'm not moving from here until you listen to what I have to say.'

'Ah, I really don't…'

'Chloe's gone. She's booked a room at a hotel in Rodney Bay and her sister is flying over for the remainder of her two-week stay. I wanted to tell you this yesterday, but I know you've been avoiding me and I didn't want to embarrass you when there were so many people buzzing around the place. I want you to know that her arrival was a complete shock. As far as I was concerned our relationship had been over for months, she was engaged to another guy, and we had both moved on. I told you that.'

'You did,' murmured Millie, clenching her palms into fists to control the rampaging emotions that had started to gallop around her body unchecked.

'However, Chloe has admitted that she lied. There was no new man in her life, no romantic proposal at the top of the Eiffel Tower. She spun me that story in an effort to make me "come to my senses" and ask her to come back. When her ruse didn't have the desired effect, she panicked, but by then I had left Oxford to come out to St Lucia.'

'So she decided to follow you here?'

'She thought that it would be like being on holiday together, forgetting that I'm actually here to work, and conveniently overlooking the fact that I had given her no reason to believe I wanted to see her, or resume our relationship. Of course, I did want us to remain friends, and she *had* travelled a long way under the mistaken belief that I still had feelings for her. I needed to explain things to her in straightforward language, but I knew I couldn't have that sort of conversation over the phone so I went to the airport to collect her. Obviously, she hadn't arranged anywhere to stay so I had to bring her back to the lodge.'

'Zach, I…'

'I know I should have handled her unexpected arrival better, but I admit that I was in total shock. I'm so sorry for my lack of communication on the ride back to the villa on Thursday morning, but I was rehearsing what I was going to say to Chloe that would let her down as gently as possible but make it absolutely clear that there could be no future for us as a couple.'

Millie wasn't aware she had been holding her breath and she tried to inhale a lungful of oxygen or she would end up collapsed into a heap at Zach's feet. His lips were inches from hers, so close in fact that she could feel his breath on her cheeks and eyelashes when he spoke. Shivers of desire rippled through her veins and out to her fingertips.

Zach heaved a sigh and ran his hand over his chin, his eyes raking Millie's face as he tried to gauge her reaction to what he was saying. She decided to let him continue his explanation without interruption to give herself the chance to formulate her own words before she spoke.

'I spent all of Thursday night consoling Chloe. She put up a good argument, I have to concede. So, in the end, I just told her that I didn't love her and there was nothing she could do to change that. The next morning when I woke up she had left the lodge and I hoped that meant that she had accepted what I'd said, but it turned out she had only taken Binks for a walk around the grounds.'

'Erm, yes. I know. Their early morning stroll took them via the villa.'

'Via the villa? You met Chloe?'

'Come on, we need to get back to the villa. I'll tell you about it in the car.'

Much to Millie's delight, Zach hooked his arm through hers and together they dashed towards where he'd left Tim's scarlet BMW Roadster, clambering in and shooting away from the hotel at speed. The breeze whipped through Millie's hair and her spirits edged up another notch as a feeling of freedom suffused her, followed by a cascade of possibilities now she knew Zach and Chloe weren't an item.

'Chloe came to warn me off.'

'Warn you off?'

'Yes, the "hands off my man" type of speech.'

'Oh my God, I'm sorry you had to hear that, Millie. I had no idea she'd been to see you. Why didn't you tell me? Ah, wait a minute, I get it now. You thought we were back together, didn't you?'

'I suppose I did. You didn't call me to tell me what was going on so I assumed… well… especially when I saw you kissing amongst the palm trees when Ella and I went down to the Purple Parrot on Friday morning.'

They had arrived at the entrance to the villa and instead of driving up the incline, Zach pulled off the road, cut the engine and turned to face Millie. His mouth twitched into that familiar smirk she had grown to love and her stomach performed a pirouette of pleasure.

'I did not kiss Chloe "amongst the palm trees" as you so eloquently put it. When you saw us, I was actually pleading with her to see sense. I thought you knew how I felt about you?'

'About me?'

Zach's eyes told her all she needed to know and suddenly she was floating on a cloud of happiness. She leaned forward and when their lips met she felt as if fireworks were exploding in the sky overhead. She had no idea how long they sat in the car, exchanging kisses and promises, but when the first of the hire cars started to overtake them, honking their horns at their romantic interlude amongst the cocoa trees, she reluctantly broke from Zach's arms and urged him to drive them to the reception before Ella and Lottie sent out a search party.

'Can we file this away under "To Be Continued"?' asked Zach, raising his eyes in mischief.

'Just you try and stop me!'

As the plantation house came into view, with its white-painted veranda and pale blue jalousie shutters, Millie let out a sigh of contentment. She glanced at the view towards the Pitons and out to the Caribbean Sea, sparkling under the sun like a sheet of dancing diamonds and dotted with flecks of white from the sails of the fishing boats. There was no other place in the world she would rather be, and no one she would rather share it with than the man sat next to her.

Before all the craziness of the wedding reception started, she sent up a missive of gratitude to her guardian angel for leading her to the Caribbean, for introducing her to such amazing and talented people, and for helping her to believe that she could love again. It was turning out to be the most perfect day in a tropical island paradise of St Lucia.

Chapter Twenty-One

'Come on! Come on! Imogen's getting ready to throw her bouquet!' cried Carla, dragging Millie out of the kitchen and across the veranda towards the steps at the front of the villa, followed by Ella and Denise and all the other women in the wedding party.

The meteorological gods had pulled out all the stops and had decided not to provide an interlude of liquid sunshine that afternoon. The whole of the cocoa plantation was bathed in a golden halo of light for the celebrations of Imogen and Alex's marriage. The courtyard, where the happy couple and their guests had just enjoyed the most spectacular wedding breakfast, was an inspired venue. Every available tree, wall, table and chair had been decorated with an abundance of fresh tropical flowers, garlands of twinkling fairy lights and Karen and Gracie's home-made butterfly bunting.

However, most important of all, everything had gone off without a hitch. The food had been delicious and the comments relayed back to the kitchen had been very complimentary. The guests were now milling around the grounds as they waited for the steel band to set up their drums and for the evening's entertainment to start.

It had been an emotional day for everyone after what they had been through, especially when, in the absence of Imogen's father, Julia had stood up to deliver a Mother-of-the-Bride speech. She'd assured the gathering that Jeff had definitely walked amongst them throughout the day, bursting with pride as his daughter made her wedding vows and how delighted he would have been to have Alex as a son-in-law.

Millie had to gulp down on the lump in her throat when she realised that, if she were ever fortunate enough to be standing in Imogen's stilettos one day, her own mother would have to perform a very similar role. Her heart gave a nip of sadness that her father would not be at her side when she walked down the aisle, but then a smile spread across her face as she realised how pleased he would be that she was able to even envisage that such an event could happen in the future, irrespective of the trauma of the past.

'Okay! Ready everyone?' called Imogen, standing on the top step, every pore of her body oozing happiness and her eyes sparkling with adoration as she glanced at her new husband standing proudly next to her. She held up the bouquet Julia had lavished such love and attention on and waved it at the section of the crowd containing all the single ladies.

'Yes!' came the cheerful chorus.

Millie glanced around the assembled crowd. There was Julia, her face alight with joy, her hand resting on Brad's arm as they watched the younger members of the wedding party jockey for the best position. Then there was Harriet, but Millie knew she wasn't interested in elbowing anyone aside to be first in line to catch the bridal bouquet because she had confided only half an hour ago that she and Owen were expecting their first child in May next year. Owen had smiled shyly at Millie, his arm slung around his wife's neck, almost too attractive for words in his crumpled linen suit and lopsided tie.

Finally, her eyes landed on Carla, bobbing and bouncing up and down in the middle of the throng, trying to position herself in the perfect spot. For the first time that day she had ditched her camera – could it be because its bulky presence would hinder her chances of catching the bouquet? She had spent the day so far snapping everyone and everything, but it was Greg who now clung onto the camera as if his life depended on it.

'Assessing the competition?' whispered Zach as he came to stand next to Millie, heart-stoppingly gorgeous in his Master of Ceremonies suit.

'No!' she giggled.

'Need any help? At times like this you might like to know that I played rugby at university. So, let's talk tactics.'

'Zach, it's just a bit of fun. A tradition, not a competitive sport.'

'Who are you kidding? I haven't seen this much gritty determination since England played New Zealand in the World Cup!'

Millie laughed as she saw Karen hoist Gracie onto her shoulders. 'I think you might be right!'

'Okay! Good luck everyone! One, two, threeee…'

Imogen spun round and threw her bouquet high over her shoulder. A very undignified scramble ensued as the female guests leapt into the air en masse, their hands outstretched as they reached for the posy of flowers. Someone shoved an elbow sharply into Millie's ribs, causing her to stumble into Zach and he snaked his arm around her waist to hold her upright.

'Can't blame your clumsy gene for that one!' Zach laughed, making no attempt to let her go.

Together Zach and Millie turned to watch the scrum taking place in the middle of the courtyard. Suddenly, there was a loud squeal of delight, as Carla emerged from the fracas victorious, hugging the now-bedraggled bouquet protectively to her chest for fear it would be wrenched from her arms.

'I wish I wasn't leaving tomorrow,' sighed Millie.

'Me too, but let's make the most of the time that's left, shall we? Enjoy every moment! Come on or we'll miss the first dance.'

Zach guided Millie back to the courtyard where Imogen and Alex were about to showcase the waltz they had been rehearsing for the last six weeks. When they'd finished, cheers and applause erupted and the dance floor filled with couples. Zach held out his hand, his eyebrows raised in question. Millie didn't have to be asked twice and, with a nod and a smile towards Lottie, who gave her a beam of approval, she moved into Zach's arms, not in the least bit surprised that her body fit perfectly into his muscular contours.

'Have you had fun today?'

'Not just today but every day since I arrived in the Caribbean. I've had an amazing adventure,

Zach, and learned a lot about myself along the way. I'm going to miss everyone.'

'Well, perhaps we could stay in touch and meet up when I get back to the UK? I should be back by the beginning of December if you want to make a date to come over to the Cotswolds for one of my legendary spag bols?'

'Sound like a plan.'

She looked up and connected with Zach's chocolate-brown eyes, fantasising about what she hoped would happen when they had the villa to themselves later that night, and enjoying the slow helix of pleasure begin its journey from her chest into her lower abdomen as their bodies moved as one to the romantic Caribbean ballad the band was playing. A waft of his citrusy cologne made Millie laugh. She had spent the whole day seeking out that reassuring aroma, knowing that it meant he would not be far away.

'What are you laughing at?' Zach asked, his mouth inches away from hers.

'Nothing,' she muttered, not wanting to break the magical spell.

As the thrum of the music changed from a waltz to the Whitney Houston classic Imogen loved, Zach's lips met hers and Millie surrendered herself to his embrace. It was a fitting end to the best day of her life.

The Paradise Cookery School

Sunshine & Secrets
Confetti & Confusion
Mistletoe & Mystery

Read on for an exclusive preview
of another novel in
The Paradise Cookery School series

Mistletoe & Mystery

Chapter One

"Oh my God! Millie, I'm so jealous! Are you sure Claudia doesn't need a fabulously talented assistant for the Festive Feast course? I could help with the reindeer cupcakes, or the gingerbread Santas, or the St Clements mince pies! And you know how much everyone loves my melt-in-your mouth shortcrust pastry!"

Millie had to smile at Poppy's enthusiasm. She really did wish she could take her friend and fellow pastry chef along with her to Claudia Croft's famous cookery school in the Cotswolds.

"In fact, scratch that. I'd even be prepared to grab my Marigolds and get stuck into the washing up if it meant I could spend the next week in Berry-ford watching Claudia show a bunch of enthusiast foodies how to rustle up a celebrity-grade Christmas feast. You are sooo lucky! Oh, and not to mention the fact that you'll be able to reacquaint yourself with that hunky estate manager you've never stopped talking about since you came back from St Lucia, the delicious Mr Zach Barker."

Millie felt the heat whoosh into her cheeks and groaned. She had been back from her trip to the Paradise Cookery School in the Caribbean for over two months, but she hadn't been able to hide her feelings for Zach from Poppy who had dug relentlessly for every scrap of detail like an overzealous gossip columnist. Nevertheless, she still wanted to make light of their imminent reunion, despite the eager anticipation that was bubbling in her stomach.

"Poppy, I'm going to Stonelea Manor to co-present the Festive Feast cookery course, not to demonstrate how to manage a country estate. I'll probably be so busy with the tutorials that our paths won't even cross."

"Who are you kidding? I've seen the photos of Zach on your Facebook page – he's *absolutely gorgeous*. If I was in your dainty sequinned sandals, I'd definitely be planning a few unscheduled visits to that cute little stone lodge he calls home, armed with a basket full of freshly baked cinnamon cookies and a bottle of home-made rum punch. Did I tell you how envious I am?"

"You might have mentioned it once or twice!" Millie giggled and rolled her eyes at Poppy as they finished wiping down the marble countertops in Étienne's, the tiny patisserie in Hammersmith where they were both fortunate enough to work.

Millie adored the atmosphere in the little café; cosy, welcoming, friendly but with a touch of Parisian elegance and the ambient fragrance of warm buttery croissants. However, for her, the best part of the shop was its bay window, hung with a necklace of red, white and blue bunting and show-casing a smorgasbord of delicious delights more akin to a high-end jewellery store – and displaying a wider variety of colours. She loved the neat rows of multicoloured macarons, of pistachio and kiwi mille-feuille, of angel wings and miniature rum babas. Every morning, she would feast her eyes on the display and declare it to be a piece of culinary art, far better than its cousins in the Tate because Étienne's patrons could *taste* their creations!

"Okay, looks like we're done for the day," said Poppy, flicking off the lights and grabbing her duffle bag. "I've got a bottle of chocolate vodka upstairs just crying out to be tested. Come on, let's go and celebrate your good fortune properly."

"My flat or yours?"

"I don't want you to take this personally, Millie, but mine – definitely. I like a bit of seasonal cheer just as much as the next person, but your living room looks like a Christmas volcano has erupted and spewed forth every decoration imaginable! Where on earth did you get all that stuff? I mean, a set of dancing pineapples in sunglasses and Santa suits?"

Millie laughed. "Got those in St Lucia – I love them! I really wanted to buy the matching set of bananas dressed as elves, but I just couldn't cram another thing in my suitcase. Maybe I should give Ella a call and ask her to ship them over for me?"

"I'm no interior decorator but take my advice and try to resist that temptation!"

Millie saw Poppy grin as she opened the door of her apartment nestled in the eaves above the patisserie and just across the hallway from Millie's own tiny studio. Poppy's flat was exactly the same size as hers, but that was where the similarities ended. The décor here reflected her friend's personality to a tee – brash, bohemian, with jewel-bedecked mirrors and lamps that Poppy had designed herself at her Wednesday night art class, a hobby chosen because it meant she could drool over the tutor – a moody French sculptor called François.

Millie sighed and collapsed down on Poppy's over-stuffed orange sofa with a surge of relief. It was the second week in December, the pre-Christmas frenzy had started in earnest, and her feet throbbed their objection to the onslaught of activity. She was already beginning to regret accepting Poppy's invitation instead of heading straight for a long soak in a hot bath filled with her favourite Moulton Brown bubbles that her sister Jen had given her for her birthday.

However, when Poppy dropped down on the seat next to her with the promised bottle of vodka and two glasses, she quickly changed her mind about the bath. She accepted a generous measure and sat back against the scarlet silk cushions, curling her legs under her bottom and taking a tentative sip of the popular liquid remedy for the weary.

"Mmm, delicious, thanks Poppy."

"So, what did your mum say when you told her you weren't going over to France for the holidays this year? Did she freak out?"

"Not when I explained why. I mean, it really is a dream come true, isn't it? Mum knows how much I loved presenting the Paradise Cookery School's Chocolate & Confetti course at Claudia's villa in St Lucia. It was a fabulous experience and I learned so much from Ella about Caribbean cooking, but now I've got this amazing chance to work with Claudia Croft herself! Poppy, I've decided that's what I want to do – present cookery classes to enthusiastic food lovers. Sooo… in the new year I'm going to start looking for a new position where I can do just that."

"And leave Étienne's?" Poppy looked scandalised, but her chestnut brown eyes were gentle and understanding. "Only joking. Millie, you could smash whatever you put your mind to. And you've no idea how happy I am to hear you say that. It's about time you moved on to new adventures – you've got a Michelin star, for God's sake. I don't know why you insist on hiding that fact."

"I'm not hiding it."

"Well, you're definitely not shouting about it from the rooftops like I would be!"

Millie watched her friend remove her sparkly hairclips and allow her hair to frame her cheeks in glossy mahogany waves. A whiff of jasmine perfume invaded the air and her heart gave a nip of gratitude for her good fortunate at having someone like Poppy in her life – she really had provided the balm to her ragged soul when she'd arrived in London having been ditched at her own engagement party.

"Actually, all that feels like ancient history now, an episode from someone else's life – someone I don't recognise."

A splash of sadness swished into her chest, but she doused it in a flash. She rarely thought of her ex-fiancé nowadays, and when she did it was with only fleeting regret, not the long, slow burn of agony that had stalked her endlessly until a couple of months ago. The way Luke had chosen to terminate their two-year relationship had hurt tremendously, but the icing on the pain-filled cupcake had been the discovery that the person he had abandoned her for was her best friend's mother. That morsel of information had been just too much to bear so she had walked out of the restaurant they co-owned, grabbed her suitcase, and ran away to start a new life of anonymity in the metropolis. Poppy had been the first non-family member she had confessed her heartbreak to and her friend had welcomed her into her world with open arms, a cheerful smile, and a surfeit of vodka in a myriad of flavours which had helped to dull the pain.

However, she was happy to report that she was done with licking her wounds. Her confidence in her culinary creativity had returned, and she was ready to launch herself into a new challenge, professional and personal. Her lips twitched at the corners when a fully formed image of the person she had to thank for her renaissance into a normal human being again appeared in her mind's eye: Zach Barker, Claudia's estate manager, whom she'd encountered at the Paradise Cookery School back in September.

Poppy was right. Zach *was* gorgeous; handsome, athletic, inquisitive, with a sharp line in sarcasm and a quirky sense of humour. Even the fact that they occupied opposite ends of the orderliness spectrum hadn't prevented them from connecting on a deeper level than she had expected. She smiled at the memory of the warm, lingering kisses they had shared beneath the swaying palm trees, with the tropical backdrop of the white beaches, sparkling blue ocean and verdant lushness of the vegetation making the whole experience seem so much more romantic.

"So, did Tim tell you why Claudia needs a co-presenter on the Festive Feast course this year? I thought she usually insists on doing all the demonstrations at her cookery school herself? After all, isn't that why most people book the courses – to rub shoulders with a celebrity? Have they accidentally overbooked or something?"

"No, there's only the usual eight fanatical food lovers booked on the course, but Tim said he'd persuaded Claudia to ask for help this year. He's worried about her. Ever since her riding accident she's been complaining about being tired all the time and Tim thinks she needs to build her strength back up after having her leg immobilised in a plaster cast for six weeks."

"And, of course, because of the fantastic job you did at the Paradise Cookery School, Claudia thought of you straight away!"

"Maybe. Anyway, he wants her to take it easy for a while – it's the perfect time over the Christmas holidays – and he plans on taking her over to the Caribbean in the new year for a blast of sunshine. He actually wanted Claudia to cancel the Festive Feast course, but she refused because she didn't want to let the students down."

"Claudia's an amazing woman," sighed Poppy, shoving a handful of home-made toffee-and-pecan popcorn into her mouth and selecting a lock of hair to twist around her fingers. "I've got all her cookery books. Hey, if I give you a couple, do you think you could ask her to sign them for me?"

"Sure," Millie laughed, draining her glass and running the tip of her tongue along her lower lip to savour every last drop. "You know, I'm really looking forward to meeting Claudia face-to-face, but I don't mind admitting that I'm also a little bit nervous. I mean, co-presenting a course with the doyenne of desserts! What if I mess up? What if…" Millie's eyes widened as she tucked an escaped curl behind her ear. "What if I smash a priceless vase or drop a bottle of vintage Krug? You know what I'm like, Poppy. Mishap Millie is what Zach calls me, and he's spot on!"

"And we've been working on those issues since you got back from the Caribbean and you're doing great," Poppy assured Millie loyally, handing her the bowl of popcorn that complimented the chocolate vodka perfectly.

"Not great! Remember yesterday when I dribbled a generous helping of crème Anglaise on the sleeve of that customer's brand-new Paul Smith sweater? It was only Étienne's swift intervention with an offer of afternoon-tea-for-two on the house that stopped him from sending over his dry-cleaning bill."

Poppy laughed as she leaned forward to refill their glasses.

"Look, Millie, you are an awesome chef. Your culinary creations will speak louder than your haphazard methods. Just use the week to learn everything you can from Claudia and when you get back you'll walk into that coveted presenting job."

"Maybe." Millie paused as something else occurred to her. "You know, Tim said something else that worried me."

"What did he say?"

"That one of the reasons Claudia didn't want to cancel the Festive Feast course this year was because it was going to be the last one."

"So that's weird. Why would Claudia want to stop running the courses?"

"I asked Tim that very question. He said it was complicated and that Claudia would explain everything when I got there, but that she's devastated. It could be one of the reasons why she's been feeling under the weather recently and has agreed to get additional help this year."

"Well, maybe you could offer your services every year from now on? Did I tell you how envious I am? Are my cheeks turning fifty shades of green? Oh, I bet Berryford is so romantic at this time of year – everything twinkling with fairy lights, the aroma of cinnamon and cloves floating through the crisp winter air, and the whole scene set to the soundtrack of White Christmas. Id–dyl-lic. Wouldn't it be amazing if it actually *does* snow?"

"No way! You know how much I hate the snow."

"Oh, but it would be the icing on the Christmas cake. A cute Cotswolds village wrapped in a soft blanket of white. A chance to sit around a blazing log fire, hugging cups of warm mulled wine, sharing bodily warmth with the local heartthrob and kissing underneath the mistletoe. Hey, Millie, maybe you should carry an emergency spring of mistletoe in your back pocket so you can whip it out when Zach's least expecting it. How can he refuse? It's tradition. Isn't that what Christmas is all about? Tradition?" asked Poppy, her dark eyes sparkling as she wallowed in her own personal version of Yuletide heaven.

Millie had to agree. Apart from the higher than average risk of snow, she adored everything about Christmas. It was the perfect excuse to fill every nook and cranny with as much festive paraphernalia as possible; tinsel, baubles, snow globes, bunting, fairy lights - her flat was stuffed to the rafters with so many decorations it looked like a hyper-active elf's grotto – and she loved it! Who would choose the stark, clean lines of Scandinavian mini-malism when you could hang a hand-embroidered snowman above the fireplace and house a whole herd of flashing reindeers on the front lawn?

Yes, she was a complete Christmas fanatic, always had been, and so was her sister Jen, much to their mother's disgust. Monique had embraced her French heritage and insisted on dressing her converted barn high in the hills of Provence with a simple fir tree and nothing else, preferring to splash her cash on all the foodie treats associated with the season – cinnamon palmiers, bûche de Noël, and a spectacular caramel croquembouche centrepiece – rather than the decorations and excessive gift-giving Millie and Jen loved so much. Millie knew she was going to *love* her week's sojourn at Stonelea Manor whipping up a long list of traditional recipes for a bunch of busy professionals.

"I wish you were coming to Berryford, Poppy. I'm not sure what Tim meant about it being the last course, but Stonelea Manor is their home, so perhaps Claudia just wants to move the school to different premises, or to concentrate all her efforts on getting the Caribbean branch properly established. I know she has plans to reinvigorate the cocoa plantation so she can make her own chocolate and offer tours of the estate to the students. That's bound to take up a lot of her time and energy."

"All the more reason for you to offer your services in the Cotswolds. And you know what the best thing about that is?"

"What?"

"You'll get to spend some real quality time with the most handsome estate manager this side of the Atlantic! It'll be the ideal opportunity to find out if the spark you both felt in the Caribbean paradise has transferred to the 'paradise' of the

English countryside. If so, then you could be on to something magical."

Despite their busy lives in different parts of the country – hers in London, Zach's in the Cotswolds now that he'd returned from St Lucia – they had stayed in touch via email and the occasional text. She was excited about seeing him again, or she had been until earlier that afternoon when she'd read Zach's response to the news of her imminent arrival; a concise text stating that they had 'a lot to talk about' when she got to Berryford – and she had no idea what that meant. Could she have misread the signals? Just in case she had, she intended to play down the fizz of anticipation bubbling through her veins.

"I'm not sure things would work between me and Zach. We *are* very different."

"Haven't you heard of the expression 'opposites attract'? And have you forgotten that cocktail-infused confession you made last Saturday night about how alive you felt whenever you were in Zach's company? But, in the event that nothing happens between the two of you – there's always the Mistletoe Ball on Christmas Eve for you to look forward to."

Millie noticed a glint of mischief in Poppy's eyes, a sure sign for her to be on her guard.

"And?"

"What do you mean?" said Poppy, all innocence.

"Poppy, I know you're cooking something up."

"Well, a little French birdie told me that François and his brother Phillipe will be there, and I might just have happened to mention that I have a gorgeous single friend with a halo of sunshine-coloured curls who's a whizz at knocking up a kaleidoscope of macarons, and who also just happens to be half-French too."

"Poppy! I can organise my own love life, thank you very much."

"Clearly not, as you haven't had a date since you got back from St Lucia two months ago. I know you profess to be over Luke, but the only way to prove it is to start dating with a vengeance. Open your heart to the possibility that there is someone amazing out there waiting to make you happy! And what better time to start than Christmas? All you have to do is trust your friendly neighbourhood Cupid and agree to a double-date with a certain chocolate-eyed Frenchman, with skin the colour of liquid caramel and a penchant for dousing himself in an excessive amount of spicy cologne."

"Poppy…"

"Look, Millie, just go to the Cotswolds, have fun at Claudia's cookery school, and if nothing happens with Zach, you can zoom back here on Christmas Eve ready to enjoy the festive season sprinkled with a little Parisian *amour*!"

Chapter Two

With the tinkle of *Frosty the Snowman* still ringing in her ears from the cab ride, Millie made her way across the concourse of Paddington Station. A curl of excitement, mingled with a generous dose of trepidation, wriggled through her chest as she contemplated what the week ahead would hold. Could she really be about to present a cookery course to eight enthusiastic foodies in the presence of the celebrity cookery book writer, Claudia Croft – in the kitchen of her fabulous manor house in the Cotswolds?

The previous night, she and Poppy had googled Stonelea Manor in Berryford and had been astonished at its picturesque splendour. Set against a Turneresque backdrop of rolling lawns and thick woodland, the Grade II listed building looked as if it had been dusted in a generous pinch of cinnamon. However, it wasn't its architectural magnificence that had caused Millie to pause and drool, but the photographs of the kitchen. She recognised it immediately from Claudia's cookery books and couldn't believe that on Monday morning she would be standing behind the marble-topped workstation issuing instructions on how to craft the perfect meringue.

A sudden blast of arctic air walloped her in the face, whipping the breath from her lips and bringing her back to the present. Goose pimples rippled over every inch of her skin and her teeth chattered uncontrollably. Much worse were the curious glances she was attracting from her fellow travellers at the ridiculous attire she had chosen to wear to brave a British winter.

She dragged the sides of her flimsy cotton cardigan around her chest, cursing the fact that she had left all her winter clothes at her sister's after the emergency evacuation from Luke's flat in April and hadn't had time to retrieve them. However, as she lived two storeys above the place where she worked, a down-filled jacket had not been high on her list of essentials, especially when there was such limited storage space. Her thoughts scooted back to her sojourn at Claudia's villa in St Lucia where she had been fortunate enough to spend some time lounging by the pool in a bikini, sipping strawberry margaritas to a backing track of reggae rhythms rippling through the sun-drenched air. Paradise!

She had always been a sun worshipper – a fact she put down to being a July baby – which was the reason she had planned to spend the Christmas holidays with her mum in Provence, even if it had meant she would have to partner her at her weekly Salsa classes.

However, the wintery temperature was a small price to pay for the opportunity to spend quality time with an accomplished chef, so Millie grabbed the handle of her wheelie suitcase and stalked towards the flashing Departures board, relieved to see that her train to Berryford was already waiting at platform three. She hitched her canvas bag higher up her shoulder, surreptitiously tapping the contents to make sure her trusty scrap box of recipes that went everywhere with her was safely stowed, and went in search of her carriage.

She selected a window seat and slumped into the corner, rubbing her palms on her thighs and blowing on her fingers in an effort to warm up. The train left on time and almost immediately she felt a veil of lethargy descend. Houses flashed by, their dark facades dotted with rectangles of amber light, highlighting the silhouettes of families gathered around the television or computer screen. As the urban sprawl melted into fields, the rhythmic rocking encouraged her to close her eyes for a few seconds, allowing her to savour the solitude of being in transit.

She must have fallen asleep because when she peeled her eyes open and glanced out of the window a bolt of shock crashed into her chest. The scene beyond the glass came directly from a Hollywood producer's demand for a typical English winter backdrop – and boy had those set designers delivered! A soft blanket of white had been tossed over the fields and rolling hills, obliterating the undulations. Huge, feather-like snowflakes fell languidly from the leaden sky, adding another layer to the wintry scene.

A glance at her watch told Millie it was almost three o'clock. Dusk was beginning to tickle the horizon with a crimson-purple hue, and the whole vista looked Christmas-card perfect, especially when a lone church spire punctured the swathe of snow reminding her of childhood Christmases when her father was still around. However, it was one thing to appreciate the scenic charm of the landscape from the comfort and warmth of a train seat, quite another to have to actually set foot in the loathsome white stuff.

A shiver cascaded down her spine as she did a mental inventory of the clothes she had stuffed into her suitcase. Feeling she should make an effort to look the part when standing at Claudia's side, she had packed her favourite Hobbs tops and a lovely crimson silk dress she planned to debut at the celebration party on the last day of the week-long course. Even if she wore every last stitch, she'd still freeze to death on her trek from the train station to the car Claudia had said she was sending to collect her. Her heart sank to her toes as the train pressed further into Oxfordshire and the gentle drift of snowflakes morphed into a blizzard. Visibility from the already opaque train window was nil.

At the nearest station to Berryford, an obliging commuter helped her to lift her luggage down from the train to the platform and she smarted at the amusement in his eyes.

"I'd put a coat on if I were you, love."

Millie glared at him for stating the obvious before bestowing him with one of the typically Gallic shrugs she and her sister Jen had inherited from their mother. Unlike Jen, who had embraced all things English when their family had relocated to her father's home town from Lourmarin, Millie still struggled with the resurgence of her French roots whenever she was stressed, angry or had overindulged on Prosecco. She had no problem whatsoever with that; she loved the trace of French in her accent that reminded her of the sunshine-filled childhood she had enjoyed in the south of France, where the necessity of owning a winter coat was non-existent.

She made her way towards the waiting room, dragging her wheelie suitcase in her wake, and lunged through the door, where, to her delight and tear-inducing relief, the central heating was on full blast. She slumped down into a seat to recover her breath and for the first time wished Claudia had decided to run her Festive Feast cookery course in her St Lucian villa high up in the hills above Soufrière, overlooking the spectacular sight of the twin Pitons, the emerald pyramids of rock poking out of the Caribbean Sea like the spines of a sleeping dinosaur.

She sprung the lock on her suitcase and grabbed another cardigan, shivering like a baby kitten and cursing her lack of forward planning. A few seconds later, her vivid stream of weather-themed invectives was interrupted by a buzz from her pocket and she fumbled with frozen fingers to answer her call.

"Hey, it's Maddening Millie! Welcome to Gloucestershire! Where are you?"

Millie rolled her eyes, but the sound of Zach's voice was like nectar to her ears. "I'm sitting in the waiting room trying to get some feeling back into my hands."

"Stay there. I'll come and get you."

A splurge of warmth that had nothing to do with the ambient temperature spread through Millie's chest as she replayed an image of Zach in his figure-hugging black tee-shirt and denim shorts as they explored the exotic sights of St Lucia together. Despite her denials to Poppy, she couldn't ignore the fact that a large part of the attraction of spending the week in Berryford was so that she would be able to spend time with Zach again. Just being in his presence made her nerve endings zing, yet she struggled to describe the relationship niche into which they had fallen. Was it friendship, companionship or something altogether more complicated? She was leaning more towards the third option and maybe spending this week together in more mundane surroundings would help her to figure it out.

A flurry of snowflakes danced in the air as an elderly couple stumbled through the waiting room door, clad in sensible fleeces, waterproof cagoules and robust walking boots with thick woollen socks turned over at the ankle. They glanced in her direction, ready to exchange a cheery seasonal greeting before performing a comedic double-take at her unsuitable attire. She gifted them a confident smile and they quickly averted their eyes.

Who in their right mind would willingly come to a place like this in the middle of a snowstorm the last week before Christmas? Millie wondered. Wasn't there an over-heated cathedral of consumerism to meander through in search of that perfect gift for Aunt Marge? In fact, if she had known she would be battling through a snow-filled Armageddon, she too might have thought twice about accepting Claudia's offer.

Within minutes, the door burst open again and her heart performed a flipflop of pleasure at the sight in front of her. Even with a woolly hat pulled down over his ears and a stylish Dr Who-style scarf wound artfully around the collar of his black denim jacket, Zach Barker was eye-poppingly handsome and her body's instant reaction to his arrival told her everything she needed to know.

Unfortunately, from the look on his face, he was clearly not thinking the same. Millie watched him run his eyes over her skimpy attire and saw his lips twitch into that familiar smirk, causing the cute dimples to appear like brackets in his cheeks, and his dark eyes to sparkle with mischief.

"I see you have come prepared for a day out at the beach instead of a journey through the snowbound countryside? What's the matter? Didn't anyone tell you it was December? Is that your luggage?"

"Yes."

"Where's your coat?"

Zach's eyes rested on her sequinned Converse trainers for a few beats before flicking back up to her face, his jaw loose with incredulity. His expression couldn't have been more amazed if she was stood before him naked.

"Erm, I didn't bring a coat. It wasn't snowing when I left London, and anyway, I plan on spending most of my time in the hi-tech *centrally-heated* kitchen of Stonelea Manor," retorted Millie, aware of the defensive note that had crept into her voice, a familiar occurrence when speaking to super-sensible Zach. "I'll be fine. Just point me in the direction of your car and I'll make a run for it."

"You've got to be joking? It's minus two out there! Here, take my jacket and channel your inner Usain Bolt. Come on!"

And before she could refuse, Zach had handed her his coat, grabbed the handle of her suitcase and jogged from the waiting room towards the car park. She rushed in his wake, slotting her arms into his still-warm jacket, revelling in the familiar fragrance of his cologne that lingered on the fabric.

When they reached Zach's car, the meteorological Gods decided to go for broke and fling everything in their armoury at them. With snowflakes lashing angrily at the windscreen like an icy carwash, Millie heaved a sigh of relief when she slammed the door and leaned her head back against the headrest.

"Urgh! I hate the snow!"

"Now why doesn't that surprise me? Don't you think it has a certain aesthetic beauty? Erasing all the sharp edges and angular gables of the ugly architecture to produce a minimalist simplicity? Oh, no, sorry I forgot, I'm talking to Amelia Harper, the Queen of Clutter and Chaos!" chuckled Zach as he struggled to steer the vehicle deeper into the countryside through the ever-increasing snow drifts.

Millie had grown accustomed to Zach's unique line in playful banter and chose not to rise to the bait. Anyway, she could see from the twinkle in his eyes and the turn of his lips that he was happy to see her.

"How far is it to Berryford?"

In reply, Zach took a sharp right-hand turn and came to an abrupt halt outside an attractive stone lodge next to a pair of magnificent carved pillars that Millie recognised from her google search as the entrance to Stonelea Manor. Visibility had improved just enough for her to get a glimpse through the windscreen of the handsome house nestled amidst a cotton wool wonderland. It was as though the property had been transported from the pages of a fairy tale and was even more beautiful than the photographs on the internet had indicated.

Apart from the honeyed stone and matching rooftiles, the building presented a pleasing symmetry, with dual mullioned windows on either side of the grand front entrance, all set against a backdrop of quite sinister woodland, a living labyrinth that could conceal a myriad of dangers. A necklace of wrought-iron lampposts meandered from the entrance gate to the front steps, but it was impossible to ascertain the precise route of the driveway.

"Why have we stopped here?" she asked, trying to ignore the squirm of apprehension agitating at her chest.

"Because, as you can see, the snow is over a foot deep and there's no way this battered old Golf will make it to the manor."

"So how are you proposing we get there?"

"We need to transfer to a more appropriate means of transport. Forward planning – ever heard of it?" Zach teased as he swung his legs out of the driver's seat and jogged around the back of the vehicle to open the boot, calling through to where Millie was still clinging to the warmth of the passenger seat. "However, even I hadn't anticipated that you'd turn up dressed for a tropical cocktail party in the Caribbean."

"I'm not dressed for…"

"Here, you'd better put these on," said Zach, tossing a jumble of cloth into her arms.

Millie scrunched up her nose in revulsion as a whiff of dead ferret, mingled with a soupçon of ammonia, invaded her nostrils.

"I'm not wearing these!"

"You will if you don't want to die of hyper-thermia."

"I think I'll risk it!" she snapped, as she unfolded the garment to reveal an ancient brown wax jacket with a dung-coloured fleece hand-sewn into the lining. It was so long the hem would probably skim her ankles.

"It wasn't a request, Millie. Put it on. The sooner we get down to the manor the better."

She reconsidered her initial diagnosis of the origins of the pungent aroma. The smell wasn't ammonia – it was linseed oil interspersed with horse manure and something else a little earthier. A hint of nausea scratched at the back of her throat.

"The hat and gloves are in the pockets."

"Is this a wind-up? Because if it is, I don't think it's very funny."

Knowing Zach's quirky sense of humour and the mischievous way he had coaxed her to experience new and exhilarating experiences in the past, Millie wouldn't have put it past him to whip out a camera as soon as she stood before him in the stupid get-up and to upload the image to his Facebook page. She scrutinised his face, a face that had frequented her dreams more often than she cared to admit, and watched him remove his hat and run his fingers through his spiky black hair then scratch at his unshaven chin; a sure sign of anxiety.

"It's not a wind-up, Millie. We've got to go – now. The weather guys are predicting one of the most severe snow storms for ten years and they're warning against all non-essential travel. We're lucky to have got this far."

"But… Oh, okay."

Heaving a sigh, Millie slotted her arms into the coat, huddling into its folds to seek out every scrap of warmth. She completed the sartorial car crash by yanking on the knitted hat and gloves and was surprised when an image of Zach's elegantly attired ex-girlfriend floated into her thoughts. She had met Chloe in St Lucia when she'd turned up unannounced to persuade Zach to rekindle their relationship, but her plan hadn't produced the result she had been hoping for and, much to Millie's relief, she'd spent the rest of her stay in Rodney Bay in the north of the island with her sister.

"Welcome to the Cotswolds, Amelia Harper. It's great to see you again," Zach whispered, leaning forward to tuck Millie's hair into the collar, gifting her with a wide grin and another delicious dash of his lemony aftershave, the soft warmth of his breath on her cheeks sending sparkles of pleasure through her frozen veins. "Come on."